EENIE, MEENIE, MINEY & MO

Best Wishes

Gilly

EENIE, MEENIE, MINEY & MO

and The Bad Badger Bankers

Gilly Horner

ISBN: 1537087339
ISBN 13: 9781537087337
Library of Congress Control Number: 2016916031
CreateSpace Independent Publishing Platform
North Charleston, South Carolina

For all the little folk

WRITTEN AND
ILLUSTRATED
by Gilly Horner

Where

In a land far away, where things are quite green
And little folk playing can often be seen,
Where flowers open petals and gaze at the sun
And bluebells jingle and join in the fun,
Where butterflies hover majestically
And jolly streams tinkle melodically,
Where hedgehogs run and roll
in the fields with glee
And the little folk are
happy as can be…
that's where it all started.

CHARACTERS

Henry Hedgehog: Henry means "home." Henry is Dad to the little hedgehogs. He is clever and wise. He likes to think he always has the last word.

Hettie Hedgehog: Hettie means "home leader." Hettie is Mum to the little hedgehogs and is very calm and caring. She lets Henry have the last word, but not always. She gets the last word in this book!

Eenie Hedgehog: She is very bright and goes to Owl School. She has even learned some turkey gobbledegook.

Meenie Hedgehog: He isn't mean at all. He is a very brave hedgehog.

Miney Hedgehog: She laughs a lot and tells some very daft jokes.

Mo Hedgehog: He is the youngest and is a bit of a dreamer. He is always up to mischief.

Dooley Badger: Gaelic. Dooley means "dark hero." Dooley is a good badger but does not think very clearly and gets mixed up. He is a very brave badger but does not realise that he is.

Benjamin (Brockies) Badger: Benjamin means "son of my right hand." Benjamin is a fine, proud, upstanding badger and is very trustworthy.

Maximus Mole: Greek/Latin. Maximus means "the greatest." He is very nosy and likes to think he is important to everyone, but he is very caring and a good friend to have.

Lilly Lapwing: Lilly means "she knows." Lilly is a symbol of innocence, purity, and beauty. She is quite bossy and likes to lay down rules. She works very hard and keeps the entire little folk well with her very good poultices.

Jenny Wren: English. Jenny means "God is gracious." Jenny is a lovely little bird and flits about singing wherever she goes. She helps Lilly Lapwing with her poultices.

Merrymouse Dormouse: Hebrew. Merry means "blithe and happy." Merrymouse is very happy and jolly looking, though she is a bit shy. She is always to be found sitting in her hedge, watching everything going on. She does not miss much.

Oscar the Otter: Norse. Oscar means "divine spear." This Gaelic derivation means "deer lover" and "champion." Oscar is a very fast swimmer, and he splashes about a lot. He is very entertaining and likes to gossip.

Drake the Duck: Greek. Drake means "dragon." Drake is a strange duck because he does not like water. Whoever heard of a duck that does not like water? The little folk eventually find out why. He is a little bit vain and likes to keep himself clean. He gets very annoyed with Oscar splish-splashing about.

Dyllis Duck: Dyllis means "genuine." She is a lovely duck whom Drake the Duck falls for.

Rasta the Rabbit: "Rasta" refers to "Rastafarian." "Ras" means "head" and "tafari" means "one who is revered." Rasta's real name is Ridgley, which means "dweller by the ridged meadow." Rasta is a nickname he gave himself because he likes dreadlocks. His ears stick up and then drop down with some dreadlocks that his cousins made for him.

Heath the Hare: Heath means "untended land." He is very manly with a very deep voice. He is a very fast runner.

Serena Swan: Latin. Serena means "calm, tranquil." Serena is a very beautiful swan. She is very graceful and has a lovely voice.

Sally Swan: Hebrew. Sally is derived from the name Sarah, which means "princess." Sally is a pretty swan and always ready to help.

Sylvie Swan: Latin. Sylvie means "from the forest." Sylvie is a strong swan and very quiet.

Squirrel Squad: Sergeant Squirrel leads the Squirrel Squad. He has an acorn whistle, and he carries a baton, which he bashes on trees when he wants attention from his squad.

Wishing Wizard: He is the Wishing Wizard because he can make some wishes come true—but not always, because he sometimes forgets how to do his magic. He also sleeps a lot and is often too late to help the little folk. He is a good wizard, and the little folk like him, but they know he is a bit dizzy.

Introduction

BIG ISLAND

Big Island is somewhere in the Atlantic, south of Greenland, not too far from England, and not too far from anywhere really. It is a lovely island with some big mountains and some not-very-big hills. It has some beautiful dales with some clear rivers and streams and becks and marshes. It has cliffs with little harbours and some big beaches. It has the greenest of grass in the greenest of fields with the greenest of hedges and trees. It even has brilliant hidey-holes for little folk. It has got everything.

It even has a Wishing Wizard.

The island is home to lots of little folk some of whom live in Rangseydale.

In Rangseydale there is a field called Slopey Field, called so because it has a gentle slope. This is where Eenie, Meenie, Miney, and Mo live. They are mischievous but lovable little hedgehogs.

Some badgers live on Big Island too, and our story begins with them. They used to live on the eastern part of the island, which was really quite low. Their setts often got water in them, so they had to move. They moved to Westshire on the west side of the island, which took a lot of doing. They would not leave behind any of the goodies that they thought were very important. At last, they thought they could be happy in Westshire.

They settled down near Rangsey Village, and they lived happily there for many years and continued to hoard lots of things in their setts. Because they were very good at this, they also provided a service to the little folk by looking after the things that they liked to collect and save. This is how they became badger bankers.

The badgers store all the deposits in specially constructed setts that they guard. The squirrels gather as many nuts as they can before winter sets in, and the birds collect special bits of nesting material. The dormice gather hazel nuts, and even the hedgehogs take some of their special chestnuts they call conkers because they love them so much. All sorts of different things are taken to the badgers, and the little folk know that they are very safe. All the badgers ask for in return is that they get to keep a very small amount for themselves.

The little folk quite like the badgers looking after their goodies and anything else that they feel like saving, and the badgers are very popular and are trusted.

Big Island

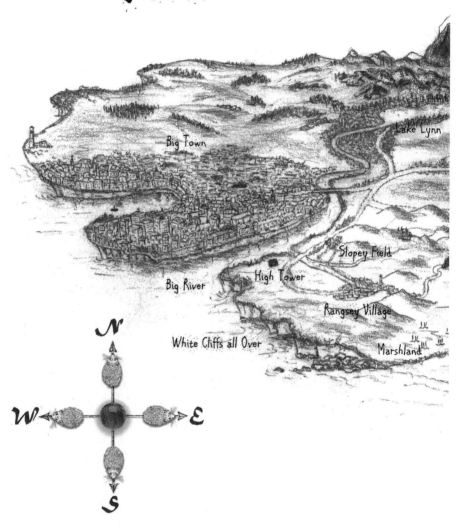

Big Town

Lake Lynn

Slopey Field

High Tower

Big River

Rangsey Village

White Cliffs all Over

Marshland

N

W

E

S

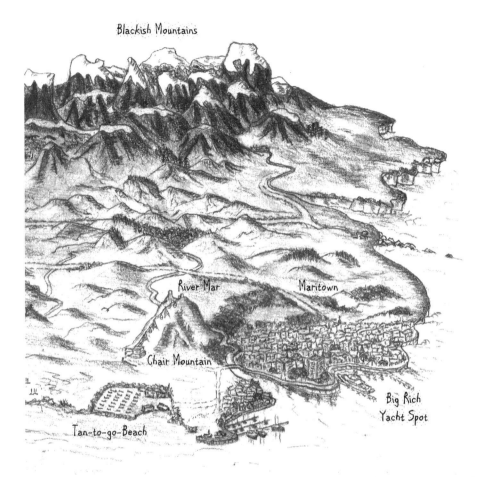

I

MANY MOONS AND STARS AGO

One winter, some very bad weather came in from the west. Great huge waves crashed into the shore, and storms raged all over Big Island, with flashing lightning and big thunder claps that frightened all the little folk.

Eenie, Meenie, Miney, and Mo were having lots of fun playing and roller bowling in Slopey Field when suddenly there was a big booming noise. Then there was another even bigger noise. Then there was some flashing and some cracking noises.

"Quick," shouted Eenie, "in here!"

And they all scurried underneath a big pile of hay and huddled together with their teeth chattering and eyes like saucers. Then it went dark, and the little hedgehogs were getting very scared. It started to rain, and rain, and rain. They snuggled together so closely that they looked like one very big spikey hedgehog with a few eyes peeking out!

In fact it rained for three whole days. Big Island had never seen a storm like this. This storm would become legendary, and it would be the source of much chattering by the little folk for many years to come.

The church steeple in Rangsey Village snapped in half and was dangling halfway down. The people had to do something quickly before it hurt anyone. In Rangsey Village, the river overflowed and flooded all the lower areas. Lots of little folk had to flee and run up the slopes to get away. Things were floating all over the village, and Drake the Duck, who did not like water, got lazy and jumped on a sofa that was floating down the main street. Because the beck was also flooded, Oscar the Otter and Drake the Duck became very confused and could not find their homes. Water was running down Slopey Field, and all the little folk got very wet indeed. In the mountains in the north were thunderstorms with lightning that had never been seen before on Big Island.

The Wishing Wizard, who usually took very long sleeps and who was known to have slept for a year once, was woken up by the noise, and he realised he must try to help all the little folk.

The badgers were suffering. Their setts were getting flooded, and some of their tunnels were also flooded. Dooley Badger had been watching the storm, and he knew that some of his family members were not very good at reacting quickly and knowing what to do in an emergency, particularly in the daytime.

Some badgers became stranded, and they could not get out; they were in very grave danger. Dooley was a very brave badger, and he went to their rescue. He saved five badgers and became a hero on Big Island. All the little folk thought he was very special.

By the time the Wishing Wizard arrived in Rangseydale, the storm had settled down, and the danger had passed. So he went back home to wherever he lived and went back to sleep.

A FEW MOONS AND STARS LATER...
When the Wishing Wizard heard of Dooley's heroics, he thought he really ought to do something special for him.

Dooley was sitting and having his breakfast one morning when suddenly, a big puff of smoke appeared out of nowhere. The Wishing Wizard swooped down and sat on his table.

"Excuse me, Wizard, but you are sitting on my breakfast," said Dooley.

"Oh, sorry, Dooley. I never was very good at landing. I hope you like squashed breakfast," said the Wizard.

"What can I do for you on this lovely morning, Wishing Wizard?" asked Dooley.

"Ah," said the Wizard, "it is not what you can do for me, but what I can do for you."

Dooley did not like riddles because they confused him, and he was not quite sure who was doing what for whom then.

The Wizard said, "I heard about all those nasty floods, and I heard about how you were very brave and saved some badgers."

"I did what I could, and I was very lucky. I was very wet and cold, but I dried out quickly. The others did not do as well because they got nasty colds for a few days."

"Well," said the Wizard, "I think that you should have a reward for being so good and clever, and I am going to give you one wish."

Wow, thought Dooley. "But I don't know what to wish for," he said.

"Think about it. I shall come back tomorrow and try not to sit on your breakfast, and I will give you your wish then." And with that, the Wizard disappeared in a puff of smoke.

Dooley pondered this all day and all night, and by breakfast time, he still had not decided. He did, however, think to put a leafy plate over his breakfast.

The Wishing Wizard casting his spell.

The Wizard arrived again, but this time he landed in a puddle. He needed to dry off before he could perform one of his magic spells, and he had brought three wands especially to do this.

"Now, Dooley, have you decided what you want to wish for?" asked the Wizard.

"Not really," said Dooley, "All I can think of is that I would love to have somewhere safe for badgers to live where we shall not run the risk of being flooded again."

"That will require some pondering," said the Wizard, and he went off for ten minutes for one of his big ponders.

"I have it!" he shouted.

"What have you had?" asked Dooley.

"I will give you a special magic tower above ground that can only be seen at night, because I know that is when you work. It can have tunnels you can build from your setts to a lift under the tower so that you can come and go as you wish and you will have somewhere safe for all badgers."

Wow, thought Dooley which he often thought when he couldn't think of anything else to think.

"It's decided," said the Wizard. He waved his arms about with a big flourish, all his wands flying about in strange spirals, and then he said some very strange words and disappeared again.

Wow, thought Dooley, again. Then he ate his breakfast and went to sleep.

That afternoon, he woke up and thought he had been dreaming. He went about his business as usual, and when it became dusk, he looked out of his sett and got the shock of his life. A big tower, standing very tall and proud in the moonlight, had appeared on the bluff on the cliff at the entrance to Big River.

Oh wow, thought Dooley, again.

Then he rushed out to tell his badger friends, and they all went to check it out.

High Tower

The badgers were all giddy, which was quite unusual for badgers. They actually ran around in circles, hugging each other and spreading glee as if it were jam on a scone. When they had calmed down a bit, Dooley said it would be a good idea to check it out, and he set off towards the tower. They all trouped after him with big, wide eyes full of wonder.

"Oh, thank goodness," said Dooley, "there is an entrance above ground. Now all we have to do is get all our tunnels to reach the bottom of the lift, and then we shall be safe."

What a novelty it was for the badgers because they had been used to the darkness of their setts. "We shall have to do something about all the windows and light," said one of the badgers.

Dooley said, "Well, the Wishing Wizard told me it would be invisible in daylight."

"What does that mean?" asked another badger "Will we all disappear? Will it be dark enough for us to sleep in the daytime? And you know very well that we do most of our work at night."

Dooley felt like a bit of a nitwit for not finding out from the Wishing Wizard. "I'll tell you what," he said very bravely, "I will stay all night. Then you can all come back, and I will tell you what happened."

"No," said the other badger, "we all want to know now, so we shall all stay." This really scared some of the badgers, but they didn't dare to speak up. Dooley himself was delighted about this because he had had jelly wobbles in his tummy when he had offered to stay on his own. He did not like jelly wobbles.

So that was the decision, and they all spent the rest of the night investigating their new home. Some of the badgers did not really like it because it was so strange, and it did not feel like home.

"Well, I think it is the bee's knees," said one badger.

"It does not look a bit like bee's knees," said another.

"It is just a phrase," said the first badger.

"It does not look like a phrase either," said the second badger.

"What's a phrase?" asked another badger.

Oh dear, thought Dooley, *I almost wish I had stayed on my own.* Then he had a rethink and decided his first thought of offering to stay was rather silly. Then he had another think and decided he was not silly. But he was having some very confusing thoughts.

I shall have to stop thinking, thought Dooley, and he decided that was a very good idea.

As dawn began to sweep over Big Island the badgers started to get restless and wondered what was going to happen. Actually, nothing happened—nothing that they could see. Everything was the same except it was light.

"I thought you said the tower would be invisible," said a badger.

"That's what the Wishing Wizard told me," said Dooley.

"Well, perhaps it is," said another badger.

"If it is, then why can we all still see everything?" asked another.

Dooley had another of his thoughts. "I think—" he said, and they all started to groan and really wished he would stop thinking. "I think," he went on, "that someone should go outside and then come back and tell us what they have seen."

"Off you go then, Dooley; we shall wait here for you."

And Dooley thought, *I've done it again, put my silly foot in it.* Then he went to the outside door, saying to himself, "I shall have to stop thinking, I shall have to stop thinking, I shall have to stop thinking, I shall..." and then he was outside all on his own.

Oh wow, thought Dooley.

He could not see the tower at all.

Oh wow, he thought again, and he stood there for ages, just staring at where the tower was supposed to be. Then he got worried about his friends. *Does that mean they have all disappeared?*

he thought. He stared at where the door should be, and he got even more worried.

He ran back to where the door should have been and bumped into nothingness. He felt around for the latch, and when he opened the door, he was back inside the tower.

Oh wow, thought Dooley, yet again.

"It's not there!" he shouted. "It's not there. I mean, it is there, but it's not."

"What dooo you mean, Dooley?" asked the bossy badger.

Dooley was beginning to get annoyed now with the other badgers and said, "Go out and see for yourselves. I am tired, and I am going to sleep. Good day." And he went off into a little corner and pulled a cardboard box over his head.

As Dooley settled down, he thought that he must rush to Slopey Field soon and tell Eenie, Meenie, Miney, and Mo about the magic tower, but he fell asleep before he had finished thinking. Eenie, Meenie, Miney, and Mo were his very best friends. He often went to Slopey Field to find out what they have been doing. He thought they were quite daft little hedgehogs, and they made him laugh.

When darkness returned, all the badgers set to work to make the tower into their new home. They rushed about, checking every area and deciding who would live where and what each room could be. After much to-ing and fro-ing and bantering and arguing, they achieved a little bit of order. Some other badgers had gone to their setts and tunnels and started to construct a tunnel underground to link to the tower.

GETTING SETTLED IN...

There were five floors, which were quite enough. The tower looked high because it was on top of the bluff at the entrance to the Big River estuary. It had one window on each floor facing different ways, but they seemed to be special windows in that they did not let a huge amount of light in, which suited the badgers.

"We shall have to decide on a name for our new home," said the bossy badger, who seemed to be taking over.

They all put their thinking looks on their faces, and no one said a thing until Dooley piped up. "I think—" And they all groaned again.

"I think we should call it High Tower," said Dooley.

"That's boring, and it's not very trendy," said a badger.

"What's trendy?" asked another.

"Here we go again," said another.

"I think," said the bossy badger, and they all stopped bantering to listen. "I think it is quite good."

"Oh yes, quite good," said another, and they all started nodding and agreeing. "Quite good, quite good."

"But," he said, and they shut up again. "I think we should call it High Tower on the Bluff, because it is high and it is on Big River Bluff."

"Right," said one.

"Right," said another.

And that's how it came to be called High Tower on the Bluff, but all the little folk shortened it to High Tower anyway.

Dooley was very happy with the outcome, and he thought the Wishing Wizard had done a very good job by making the tower.

II

A NEW DAY

Slivers of light were appearing as Dooley opened his eyes. Then he shut them very quickly because he thought he was dreaming. He opened one eye very slowly and saw that he hadn't been dreaming. He jumped up very excitedly. *Wow,* he thought for the umpteenth time. *I had better go and tell my friend little Mo and his brother and sisters about this brilliant news.* And he dashed out of the door. As he went through the door, he braked suddenly, nearly tripping over himself. He looked back over his shoulder and saw nothing. "Gosh, wow, gosh!" he said out loud, and then he ran as fast as his legs could carry him, even though it was daylight and badgers don't really like to be out in the sunshine.

Dooley rushes to Slopey Field to tell
Eenie, Meenie, Miney, and Mo his brilliant news.

Now, this was very unlike Dooley. He usually woke from his very many sleeps in a slow and laborious way that made you think he might just fall asleep again before he had actually moved. Then he would wiggle his butt slowly and make a determined effort to stretch, which tired him out, and sometimes it tired him so much that he did go back to sleep. If he did manage to wake up, then he would trundle along with his nose to the ground, just in case he found some food. Today was different. Dooley wasn't going for one of his trundle walks; Dooley was on a mission.

As he got near Slopey Field, he could see the little hedge-hogs stirring. "Eenie, Meenie, Miney, and Mo, wake up!" he shouted as loudly as he could, and he arrived in a flurry, scattering hay all over the place.

Henry Hedgehog said in as deep a growly voice as he could muster, "What on earth is all that noise about?"

"I have some wonderful news for you all; it is really quite magical. You won't believe it, but it's real. It really, really is real!" he said, jumping up and down like a Ping-Pong ball.

"What on earth are you talking about?" asked Henry as Hettie Hedgehog poked her nose out of the hay to tell them off for being so noisy.

Eenie, Meenie, Miney, and Mo all got up to find out what all the excitement was about.

"The Wishing Wizard has done it. It is spectacular when you can see it, but you can't see it all the time," gushed Dooley.

Hettie was getting quite annoyed by then, and she told Dooley off. She told him to sit down and start at the beginning. So he did. It took him all morning to tell it, and all the hedgehogs just sat and stared at him in wonder as he told his tale.

"Harrumph," said Henry. "That sounds most improbable; you have a very vivid imagination, Dooley."

"But it's true," protested Dooley. "I can show you, but you will have to wait until the sun is going down."

"It won't do any harm, Henry, to check out what Dooley is telling us," said Hettie.

Mo piped up, "Can we all go, please, please, please?"

"Oh, all right," said Henry, who always had the last word.

So they all set off in one line, crocodile fashion. By the time everyone was actually ready to set off, it was a very long line indeed, because lots of other little folk had tagged on to see what all the fuss was about. They had to go to the bottom of the field, under the farmer's gate, and along the big road bridge. Henry told them all to stick together and wait until he said it was safe for them to cross the bridge.

When they arrived at High Tower, they stopped, and Miney said, "Well, where is it this fancy tower then Dooley?"

"Have patience; you will see it soon," said Dooley.

So they waited and waited, and eventually they all started getting restless and jumping about. They were beginning to think Dooley was a bit daft.

Then, when the sun began to go down, they all stopped and gawked, which means their eyes went very wide, their mouths opened, and they all said, "Oh wow," at the same time. The tower was beginning to appear.

"Well," said Henry to Hettie, "what do you make of that?"

"No good can come of it, Henry," she said.

Hettie turned to Dooley and said, "What about our goodies that the badgers are looking after? What will we do now? Are they still going to look after all our goodies?"

Dooley said that not all the badgers had come to High Tower, and he thought that the Brockies did not want to move in. Benjie Brocklehurst was happy where he was, and he said they had the best-constructed setts on the island. Dooley told Hettie that he would find out and let her know.

He was a bit upset that that Henry and Hettie did not seem as impressed by the tower as he was.

The little hedgehogs were all jabbering away about how the tower was not there and then how it began to appear, and Hettie was beginning to get a headache. Henry told them all to be quiet and said they would have a good talk about it to-morrow. They were all very tired, and all the little hedgehogs started a competition to see who could do the loudest yawn.

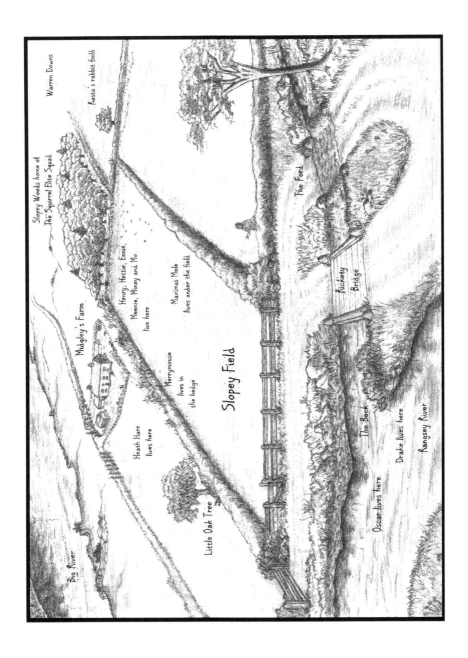

ANOTHER DAY BEGINS

Henry Hedgehog and his family all sat down to talk about what they had seen the day before. The little hedgehogs thought the tower was really special and wanted to go again to see it disappear. Henry said they could not go again because they would have to get up very early.

They all thought about High Tower, decided that it probably would not make any difference to them, and settled down to play.

Maximus Mole was watching the antics of Henry's brood because he felt it was his duty to keep an eye on them, but he too was a bit concerned about what they were talking about.

Maximus is the underground keeper of Slopey Field because he has lots of mole tunnels. He had been very busy the previous evening, and there was much evidence of his work; little piles of earth dotted all over the field like fruit pudding. He is a nosy little mole and likes to know everything that is happening. He does not miss much and keeps his tiny ears to the ground, so to speak. He wears spectacles that one of the little folk found. They are held on with little pieces of dock leaf, with a drop of special sticky lotion that Lilly Lapwing makes. He is a very clever little mole and is like a mole on a motorbike when he takes off—and a happier little mole you would have to go a long way to find, even though he is very good at muttering to himself. He detects movement through vibrations, and Henry's brood were causing too many vibrations. That made him grumpy.

Maximus Mole keeping his eyes on things.

Miney got her marbles out to play with, but it was not long before they were all arguing.

"I'm not playing anymore!" said Miney, stamping her little paw in disgust. "You're cheating!"

"I'm not cheating; you are not very good at marbles, and you are a spoilsport." Meenie said.

"I am not," Miney shouted. "You are pushing the marbles and not flicking them as you should. I am going in to count all the rest of my marbles. You're just a big cheat."

Mo started roller bowling as usual.

At this point, their dad, Henry, intervened. "Stop that silly noise."

"But he's cheating, Dad."

"No, I'm not," said Meenie.

"Right, that's it. If I hear any more from you two, I will take all your marbles off you," said Dad.

Miney marched away in disgust. Her sister and brothers were now rolling about in the hay, playing at real marbles and rolling into each other. This was the usual game at this time of the year for Henry Hedgehog's family. They had a lot of fun after hay making, and the young hedgehogs could make hiding places all over the field.

While all this was happening, Maximus Mole was getting quite frustrated by the stamping that was going on above him. He really wished Henry would sort out his youngsters. It was hard for him to concentrate on where he was going with all that noise.

All was quite normal on that summer evening in Rangseydale, or so most folks thought.

Merrymouse the dormouse, who lives in the hedge that runs down the side of Slopey Field, was watching all the jollities with a huge grin on her face. She knew that wherever Henry Hedgehog's family was, there was always a bit of food left over for the likes of a little mouse like her.

"Stop roller bowling, Mo," shouted Eenie. "It is dangerous!"
"Oh, oh, I can't stop!" shouted Mo.

The hedgehog children were quiet for a while, and Eenie started daydreaming.

Miney started stringing her beads, which were dried-out acorns from last autumn.

Meenie stuck his paw in his mouth and just watched his brother and sisters, and then he began to fall asleep.

Mo, still grumpy, rolled up again and started bowling around just to annoy everyone.

Miney chuntered that her acorns were all a bit boring because they were not very colourful, but everyone just ignored her, apart from Eenie, who just raised one eyebrow and smiled.

Slowly, they all settled down to have a nap. Hedgehogs are good at that.

In this very moment of peace and tranquillity, Heath the Hare blasted through under the branch that Merrymouse was balancing on, nearly shaking her off. Merrymouse was sure he must be in training for something because he was getting faster and faster. He left a draught in his wake, and that certainly would not do on a lovely summer day. *Maybe he was going to run in a race*, Merrymouse thought.

Then Merrymouse went to sleep. She too was good at going to sleep. The following day, life for the little folk continued as usual.

Heath runs by, scattering grass everywhere.

JULY BEGINS

It was now July, and the little folk had been storing their best possessions with the Brockies all spring and summer. They knew they would have to get some back as winter would be coming soon. Henry and Hettie had to start preparing for their winter hibernation, and they all set to work to make sure they would be comfortable when the time came for them to go to sleep.

Eenie, Meenie, Miney, and Mo were up to their usual antics of playing at roller bowling.

Eenie was lying on her spines and looking up at the sky, watching a plane go by, and suddenly she said, "I want to be a pilot when I grow up."

"What's a pilot?" asked Mo.

"It's someone who flies," said Eenie.

"You can't fly; you haven't got any wings," said Mo.

"No, in a plane, dummy."

"A dummy is something human blings give their babies to put in their mouths," said Miney.

"It's not human blings; it is human beings," said Meenie as usual and was totally ignored. As usual.

"Does a dummy taste good?" asked Mo.

"No, it is not food," said Eenie.

"Then why do they put it in babies' mouths?" asked Mo.

"To keep them quiet," said Eenie.

"Human blings are very strange," said Miney.

Meenie shouted, "It's not human blings; it's human beings."

"I like calling them blings; it suits them," Miney said, knowing full well that she had always thought they were "blings" until Meenie told her otherwise.

"You know, I wish someone would make Meenie shut up," said Mo.

With a big sigh and a big drop of his shoulders, Meenie said, "Oh—I thought I was helping." And he slunk off, looking very sad.

"Oh heck, now look what you've done," said Eenie.

Hettie Hedgehog came to them at this point and asked, "What is the matter?"

They went very quiet, and then they all said together, "Nothing, Mum." They dropped on all fours and ambled quietly away.

They all seemed to have forgotten High Tower, probably because they found it hard to believe anyway.

Maximus Mole was shovelling some soil out of one of his tunnels and said, "How is a good little mole going to be able to carry out his very important duties if he has to listen to this every day?" But no one was listening to him. He was grumpy because his little glasses annoyed him at times, even though they helped him see, because one of the dock-leaf plasters that held them on was about to drop off. He knew that if Lilly saw them, she would send Jenny Wren down with another one, and he could not be bothered with her fussing, so he ducked his head down quickly.

Lilly Lapwing, with Jenny Wren's help, gathers all sorts of herbs to make special healing potions. She puts some of the sticky mix on little pieces of dock leaves. These are their poultices, and they store them with the badgers until they need them. The poultices are very good, and whenever any of the little folk get hurt, Jenny Wren swoops down and sticks a poultice on the bit that hurts. They are used for any ache and pain as well as cuts, grazes, and even toothaches and headaches. They cannot be pulled off and stay on until they drop off.

**Lilly Lapwing and Jenny Wren
prepare a new batch of poultices.**

III

MERRYMOUSE GOES TO THE BECK

Merrymouse had also been watching the little hedgehogs, and she decided she would go for a walk just to get some peace and quiet.

So she went for one of her weekly jaunts. She did not go very often because she was such a little mouse that, it was hard work for her to go very far. She decided to go down to the beck to see if anything was happening. She wasn't the bravest of little folk when it came to water because it was a bit cold and wet, and it kept moving. But it did fascinate her.

When she finally arrived at the water's edge, she could not see anyone and all was quiet. However, she did see a white cup floating in the water. Merrymouse thought, *I would really like to know what it feels like to float on water like Drake Duck and Serena Swan.* She looked around to see if she could find anything to help her get the cup to the side of the beck. She found a short stick that she could only just manage to lift and pushed it towards the cup. She knocked it on the side and slowly nudged it towards the bank. Not known for being very brave, when she stuck one paw on the side of the cup and it wobbled, she jumped back in fright. She was a bit annoyed that this little cup was hard to move, but as she was still inquisitive, she pulled the cup back towards her and tried again. This time she managed to climb into the cup, and it started edging away from the bank.

"Oh, oh, what have I done?" whimpered Merrymouse, her eyes huge and scared. She hung on to the side of the cup, and little tears began to fall from her eyes.

The cup started to go round and round, and she began to feel a bit sick. "I want my mum," she said and started to cry.

Drake the Duck had been watching her antics from the other side of the beck and waiting until he thought Merrymouse had learned her lesson. Even though it meant getting wet, he swam over towards her.

Drake lives on the beck and the river. He sometimes brings other ducks just to show off the beck. He has a secret, though—he is probably the only duck that does not like water. He does not like to get muddy or wet, even though he has to because that's what ducks do. Watching Merrymouse, he decided this was one occasion when he would have to get wet.

"What is the matter, Merrymouse?" asked Drake.

"I am a daft mouse and thought I would be able to swim like you on the water," said Merrymouse. "Please, please, will you help me?"

Drake the Duck put his huge beak on the rim of the cup and pushed it towards the bank. "Oh, thank you, Drake, you are the best duck in the world," said Merrymouse.

"I know that," said Drake Duck as he stuck his beak in the air. As he started to swim away, it crossed his mind that Merrymouse might have heard something about the badgers.

"Merrymouse, have you noticed anything unusual lately?" asked Drake.

"In what way, Drake?" asked Merrymouse.

"Well, I know you hear all sorts of things and wondered if you'd noticed if the badgers were doing anything unusual," he said.

"Not really, other than I have seen some out in daylight, and that is a bit strange," said Merrymouse.

"Mm," said Drake as he swam away to dry off.

Merrymouse thought that was really quite nice of Drake to do what he did, because he was not usually a very friendly duck. She did, however, wonder why he was asking questions.

When Merrymouse got back, Eenie saw her and noticed she was a bit upset.

"Whatever is the matter, Merrymouse?" she asked.

"Oh, nothing," said Merrymouse, not wanting to admit she had been a silly mouse. "I have been down to the beck and feel a bit tired."

Merrymouse is very worried about being adrift in the beck.

IV

RAINBOWS

Meanwhile, back in Slopey Field, all the little folk had heard about High Tower, and they thought it was very kind of the Wishing Wizard to do what he did. They thought he might do good things for them too, when he got around to it.

Now it was the middle of August, and it had been raining in Rangseydale. Slopey Field was quite wet, but the little folk were beginning to venture out again.

"Oh, look," said Miney, "there is a rainbow over there."

"Cool," said Mo; he copied Rasta Rabbit whenever he could. "I like rainbows. I wish we could have one all the time."

"It is very pretty," said Mo. "Where do all the colours come from?"

"Oh, that is a big question," said Eenie.

"When the light changes, they go away, but they come back another day," said Eenie.

"Oh, that is clever, Eenie; you are a poet," said Miney.

"Eenie is a poet! Eenie is a poet!" sang Mo.

Rasta Rabbit, who lives in a field just above Slopey Field, bobbed over when he heard Mo singing. Rasta is Mo's hero. He has some dreadlocks on his ears that one of his cousins made for him. Mo loves his dreadlocks.

"What are you singing about?" asked Rasta.

"Eenie is a poet, and I like rainbows," said Mo.

"Cool," said Rasta as he hopped away. "I'll spread the word," he said.

"What word?" asked Mo, totally confused, and they all settled down for a very short nap.

Mo tells his hero Rasta that Eenie is a poet.

When they all woke up, Miney asked her mum, "Can we all go down to the beck?"

"You can," said Hettie, "but remember that it has been raining, and the beck will have faster-running water in it. So do not go too near the bank."

So off they all trotted in a straight line, with Eenie up front followed by Meenie, Miney, and Mo. They had to keep waiting for Mo to catch up because he kept stopping when something took his fancy. He liked watching the butterflies, and he would stick his little snout in the air and wave it about as he followed the butterflies flitting about over the flowers.

Eenie decided to make it a longer walk and took them up to Midgley's farm first.

"Oh, look, Eenie, there is that funny-looking bird that I saw last week," said Mo.

"He really is a funny-looking bird; what's his name?" Meenie asked.

"Turkey," said Eenie.

"Oh—what's he talking about?" Miney asked.

"He talks gobbledegook," said Eenie.

"What's 'gobbledegook'?" asked Mo.

"It's what turkeys talk," said Eenie.

"What's it mean?" Meenie asked.

"Well, I can make a bit of sense of it, but it is not easy," said Eenie, getting really fed up with answering their questions.

"I thought you knew everything," Meenie joined in, "because you go to Owl School two times a week."

"Not all gobbledegook—only turkeys know all gobbledegook."

"I still thought you knew everything," Meenie said.

"Oh, I wish you would all shut up!" shouted Eenie as she lost her temper, which was quite unusual for her.

And they all shut up for a very, very short time and then started talking about that wonderful rainbow they had seen.

Then Mo mentioned High Tower. "I wonder how the badgers are getting on," he said.

Then Miney said, "I don't like High Tower."

Mo said, "Why? Is something the matter?"

"They are different now. The badgers are not as nice as they used to be. I think something is going on, and I don't know what!" she pronounced quite loudly.

This made all the hedgehogs think very hard, and then they all started to fall asleep.

V

TRIP TO RANGSEY VILLAGE FOR JAM

"It's time to go on a foraging expedition to Rangsey Village again," said Meenie the next day. "Our stocks are running low, and we do not have much saved with the Brockies."

"What does foraging mean?" asked Mo.

"It means searching for and collecting things that we need," said Meenie.

"Yes," said Miney, "we haven't had any jam for such a long time; let's go."

Eenie said, "Right, that's settled, then. Off we jolly well go!" And off they jolly well did. They were always jolly when jam was on their minds.

Rangsey Village is the quaintest of villages that could ever be imagined. A stream joins the river that runs right along Main Street, with hundreds of pretty flowers on its little banks in the summertime, and there are little bridges to walk across it to get to the other side.

Many tourists visit Big Island in the summer and often stay in Maritown, and they visit Rangsey Village. There is a pub, which serves food. There is a café, which the local people call "the caff." It also serves food. And, last but not least, there is a bigger café called "Cosy Teapot," which also serves even more food! Wherever there is food, there are bins with food that has been thrown away. This was good for the little folk because they could go foraging. Eenie, Meenie, and Miney often went on these trips, but Mo did not always go because he was a bit of a dawdler.

Eenie, Meenie, and Miney would creep up to where the bins sat, outside all the buildings where people ate food. People threw lots of good stuff away. The very best place to go was the Cosy Teapot Café because there were often a few little jam pots that had been thrown away that still had lots of jam in them. If they managed to find any that had not been opened, then that was treasure trove!

They trundled down to Main Street, keeping very quiet, and as soon as they sighted the Cosy Teapot, they could see lots of rubbish outside. "Oh this is going to be a good forage," said Miney. And it was.

On the way, they passed a little shop window, and Miney said, "Look, that's that shop that has walking sticks that have little folk heads on them; I think human blings are really strange."

"It's not human blings; it's human beings!" shouted Meenie.

"That's enough," said Eenie. "It is silly to keep on arguing about this; human blings are silly anyway."

And Meenie said, "You said that on purpose; I think you are all silly too." And he did a big sulk.

They arrived at the back of the Cosy Teapot and found lots of things to collect. Meenie stopped sulking when he saw all the jam pots.

Loaded down with whatever they could carry or drag along, they set off back to Slopey Field. It took them quite a while with so much to take back.

When they got back, Mo jumped and clapped his little paws. "Oh, goody! Look how much jam they brought back, Daddy."

"Now, don't be greedy," said Meenie, who was not a mean hedgehog at all; he just liked things to be fair.

Miney soon had a very red face, and it was not from blushing; it was from raspberry jam juice from the jam pots. The rest of the hedgehogs soon cleaned her up as they licked her face!

"Scrummy," said Meenie.

"Charmed, I'm sure," said Miney.

And they all fell about laughing, which they did quite regularly.

Mo was soon full up with jam, and he had sticky red blobs on his whiskers. He started singing.

"Yummy, yummy, yummy, I've got jam in my tummy, and I feel it's a really special day. Yummy, yummy, yummy, I've got jam in my tummy, and I feel it's a really special day."

It was a bit repetitive, but Mo did not know how to make up many singing words.

**Meenie and Miney gather lots of jam pots at the Cosy Teapot
while Eenie keeps watch.**

Later that day, Mo went up to the top of Slopey Field in
the hope of seeing Rasta Rabbit in his field. He took with him
one of the carrots that Meenie had carried back from their expedition. When he got there, he could see Rasta, and he was
singing. *What on earth is he singing about*, thought Mo, and he
decided not to disturb him.

When he got back, he said to his mum, "I just saw Rasta
Rabbit, and he was singing about jam."

His mum said, "It's a funny thing to sing about."

"'Well, it was something with jam in it anyway," said Mo.

"Ah," said Hettie Hedgehog. "He's heard human beings singing about that," she said.

Oh, thought Mo, *they must like jam as much as hedgehogs*, and with that, he started humming his little jam song.

Henry and Hettie with Eenie's help started to sort which goodies they were going to keep. The rest they would take to the badgers to store.

Mo asked his dad, "When I was talking to Rasta the other day, he told me he thinks something is going on at High Tower. Is it still OK to take our goodies there?"

"Oh," said Miney, "Merrymouse has said that she too thought something was not right."

"I shall look into it. But I think everything will be all right," said Henry.

Hettie was not quite so sure because there were a few little folk talking about the badgers.

VI

SOMETHING IS DEFINITELY
GOING ON

Most of the little folk were soon used to High Tower being there at night, and some of the badgers looked after their goodies in the tower. All the excitement seemed to have settled down, and Hettie began to relax a little and thought that perhaps the Wishing Wizard had been right for once. She did not have a huge amount of faith in the Wishing Wizard, mainly because he was never around when he was needed, and he tended to sleep too much. She could not say anything, though, because hedgehogs go to sleep for the winter anyway.

Today Eenie, Meenie, Miney, and Mo all decided to go to the beck again just to see who was around. When they reached the bottom of the field, they spotted a scarecrow propped up in the bottom corner of the next field.

Miney said, "He must be having a rest because he is not in the middle of the field."

"Scarecrows are not needed at this time of the year," said Eenie.

"Why?" asked Mo.

"Because they are only put in the fields to frighten the birds away, to stop them from picking and eating all the seeds that have just been planted by the human beings in spring."

Eenie went on. "Because scarecrows cannot move, human beings have to put something on a scarecrow that will move; otherwise it does not work as well, and it does not frighten the birds away."

"I don't understand," said Miney.

"Well, if a scarf is put round the scarecrow's neck, then it will flutter in the wind, making movement that will frighten the birds," said Eenie.

"Oh, that's clever," said Meenie, even though he did not think human beings were clever at all.

So they went on their merry way with Mo last in the line as usual, and just as they were leaving, the old scarecrow winked at him.

"Oh," shouted Mo, "he winked at me."

"Don't be daft, Mo; he is not real. He is just stuffed to make him look like one of those human blings" said Miney.

"It's not human blings; it's human beings," said Meenie.

"He did too; I saw him!" shouted Mo.

"Can't have," said Eenie.

"Can't have," said Meenie.

"Can't have," said Miney.

"Did too," said Mo, and he had a big sulk. He did not sulk for long because he soon forgot what he was sulking about.

When they reached the beck, they saw Oscar the Otter splish-splashing, and Drake was behind some reeds trying to keep dry.

Oscar is a very lovely otter, very sleek and athletic. If ever any little folk want a natter with someone, they can rely on getting one from Oscar. He does, however, have a habit of swimming away in the middle of conversations, and it leaves some folk a bit confused.

"We can see you, Drake; you can't hide from us," shouted Meenie.

"I'm not hiding. I am just trying to keep dry," said Drake. "Oscar is splashing all over."

"I think you are a daft duck, Drake," said Eenie "Whoever heard of a duck that doesn't like water?"

"It is not the water I don't like; it is the mud. I like to keep clean," Drake said.

"You will never be as white as Serena Swan," said Miney, and Drake the Duck started going slightly pink.

Ah, thought Eenie, *Drake has a liking for Serena. That's why he tries to keep clean and off the water. Now it all makes sense!*

"Are you blushing, Drake?" asked Miney. "I didn't know ducks could blush."

"Hush," said Eenie, "Don't be mean."

Oscar did not miss any of this and said, "Serena Swan should be swimming down to visit us before long, because she hasn't been for a while." And Drake went even pinker, paddled into the water, and swam away.

"Stop splashing, Oscar!" shouts Drake.

"Now look what you've done," said Meenie. "You daft old otter."

"I am not old," said Oscar. "Not yet, anyway." He splish-splashed getting them all a bit wet.

"Did you hear about High Tower, Oscar?" asked Mo.

"I did, and I reckon it might not be a good thing," said Oscar.

"Why not?" asked Meenie.

"Well, the badgers all seem to be splitting up into groups and doing a lot of whispering, as if they are not all friends anymore."

Oh, thought Eenie *I'd better tell Dad about this.*

Meenie said, "Well, why don't you try to find out what's going on, then, Oscar?"

"That is not a bad idea, Meenie. I will do some research."

Meenie was proud that Oscar had thought this was a good idea, and Mo asked, "What's 'research'?"

They all groaned loudly.

"Eenie, when you were talking about the scarecrow and you said that when the scarf blew in the wind it scared the birds away, well, what if there is no wind?" asked Miney.

"Then the farmer has to hope that the birds do not get wise and realise the scarecrow is not a real person, because then they won't be afraid, and they will eat the seeds that he has planted."

"Is hope good, then?" asked Miney.

"Oh, yes, everyone needs it," said Eenie.

Just then Heath the Hare blasted in and skidded to a stop. He was panting so much that he had to get his breath back before he announced, "The badgers are up to something."

"We already know," said Miney.

Heath plonked down on the ground and looked crestfallen. "How do you know?" he asked in his deep gruff voice.

"Well..." And then they all started talking at once.

Heath was feeling very confused by all the babbling, and Maximus Mole poked his head up and shouted as loudly as he could, "Shut up!" And they all stopped and stared at Maximus.

"You are all making too much noise and not giving yourselves time to think." So they all sat thinking.

After a while, Meenie said, "We should do something, but I don't know what."

Eenie said, "We should tell Mum and Dad; that's what we'll do." And they did.

Mo scampered away, shouting, "Dad, Dad!" And they all followed.

"Now then, Mo, what's the matter now?" asked Henry, who liked saying "Now then."

"Well—" And they all started talking at once again. So Maximus Mole once more shouted, "Shut up!"

Merrymouse was watching all this and squeaked, "Oh dear, oh dear," as she did very often.

Lilly Lapwing and Jenny Wren flew down to see what all the commotion was. Jenny saw Merrymouse, and she flew into the bushes to say hello. They started playing a game of hide-and-seek.

Jenny could not count, but she knew some numbers. So when it was her turn to seek, she said, "One, seven, nine, ten, twenty, eight, six. Ready or not, I'm coming!" They skittered up and down the hedge, making daft noises, while the hedgehogs and Maximus Mole talked about the badgers.

"Give in," squeaked Merrymouse. "You'll never find me!"

VII

RASTA SHINDIG

It was now the end of August. Mo had been out on one of his jaunts, and he came back with a very worried look on his face.

"What's the matter, Mo?" asked Eenie.

"I have just been down the field, and Maximus Mole has moved to the bottom of the field because all the latest mounds that he shovelled out are all down at the bottom. What does that mean?" asked Mo.

Eenie did a big ponder and suddenly said, "I know. Don't you remember, Mo? Last year Rasta Rabbit had a shindig, and all his friends came to his field. They had lots of fun."

"What's a shindig?" asked Mo.

"It is just a fun get-together with music and stuff, I think," said Eenie.

"That sounds good," said Mo. "I think I'll go up and take a look."

"Well," said Eenie, "you had better get up early, because they start as soon as the sun rises and keep going until the afternoon when they all get tired and go home."

"Cool," said Mo.

"I want to come too," shouted Meenie.

Mo and Meenie woke up just in time to get themselves up Slopey Field to watch Rasta's shindig.

They settled themselves down to watch just outside the fence.

"Oh, look," said Mo, "at all those rabbits dancing at the other side of the field."

Rasta heard him and said, "That's the *topsy-turvy* dance, Mo."

"I would like to do the *topsy-turvy* dance," said Mo.

"You had just better watch them for a while," said Meenie, "then decide."

So Mo watched.

The little rabbits clapped their front paws together, which made a sound like "clap, clap." Then they stamped each back leg in turn, which sounded like "bang, bang," They skipped and kicked first one leg and then the other making a "shuffling" sound. Then they rolled forward, making a "swishing" sound, and waved their back legs in the air while their tails bobbed up and down. This sounded like "bleeeeee, bleeeeee."

Then they rolled upright and started it all again!

The whole thing sounded like

Clap, clap,

Bang, bang,

Shuffle, shuffle,

Swish, swish,

Bleeeeee, bleeeeee,

Shuffle, shuffle.

Rabbits having fun doing the rabbit dance.

Because the rabbits kept moving forward all the time, they had to do their *topsy-turvy* dance round the outside of the field, and any rabbit could join in at the back. The effect was quite funny and looked like lots of fun. Mo was very keen to have a go.

So Mo had a go—at least he tried to. He managed the clapping and stamping, but when he rolled forward, he couldn't stop. He bowled into some rabbits, sending them sprawling.

"Oh, Mo, watch out, you silly hedgehog. This is a rabbit dance, not a hedgehog dance; you should make up your own dance," said one of the rabbits, who was nursing a sore ear, which Jenny Wren was already putting a poultice on!

"Oh, sorry," said Mo. "That's not a bad idea." He sat down to do a big ponder. He was still thinking about his hedgehog dance when Meenie said it was time to go. He was a bit disappointed, but it gave him lots to think about over the next few days. He bored his brother and sisters with all his dance talk.

While Mo had been watching the dancing, Meenie had been talking to some of Rasta Rabbit's friends, and they said they were worried about something. Meenie, who liked to think he could help anyone, asked them what the problem was.

"Well," said Robbie Rabbit, "when we were over near Midgley's farm, we heard the turkeys talking. Tittle Turkey and Tattle Turkey said they had seen some badgers the previous night, and luckily, the badgers had not noticed them. Tittle and Tattle could hear what the badgers were saying, and it was a bit worrying even though they did not understand it."

"Hurry up, Robbie; tell us what they heard!" said Meenie, who was getting quite agitated.

"Well, it was generally about getting together next year in April in Slopey Field," said Robbie. "I could not quite work out all that they said because, as you know, turkey talk is not easy."

Meenie was so upset that he ran as fast as a little hedgehog could back to see his dad. He arrived in a flurry and skidded into Miney, who fell and hurt her head. "Put a poultice on it!" shouted Meenie.

Jenny Wren was on the case straight away, and poor Miney was stuck with a poultice on her forehead. Jenny Wren could see something was not right, so she stayed in the hope that she could listen to what was going on.

Henry sat both Meenie and Miney down, and Hettie calmed them down.

"Right, now you can tell us what the matter is, Meenie," said Henry.

Meenie told his dad all about what he had heard. Henry knew that this might be serious and that he really ought to call a general meeting in Slopey Field.

"Right," said Henry. "I shall look into this. When I have an answer, I shall speak to you all again, and in the meantime, you should not worry." Except Henry was worrying, and he did not want them to know.

The following day, Henry had all his brood get together so he could tell them that they were to keep their ears to the ground.

"What does that mean?" asked Mo.

"It means listen for any strange talk or any secrets," said Meenie.

VIII

RASTA AND THE SQUIRREL SQUAD

The following day, while Rasta was having one of his very rare walks in the Slopey Woods, he noticed that there were not many squirrels running around. He looked up into the trees and saw a strange sight. All the lower branches of some of the trees had squirrel tails hanging down. *What on earth is going on?* he thought. He crept closer underneath them and could hear some of the squirrels talking. Luckily, he was quite good at working out squirrel talk, but he was a bit concerned because they did not sound very happy.

On his way back to Slopey Field, he tripped over a Maximus Mole mound. Maximus had just burrowed out and created a big lump of soil, and Rasta tumbled over it.

"You daft mole," said Rasta. "You should look where you are going."

"How can I look where I'm going when the soil is in front of me? You should look where you are going!" he shouted.

"What's all that to do about?" asked Mo, who was having a fun roll-about.

"Rasta is bad tempered today," said Maximus.

"I am a bit worried about what is going on in the woods," said Rasta. "All the squirrels are up in the trees in a huddle, but they've all got their tails hanging down, which is very strange."

"Oh dear," said Maximus, and he burrowed back down into the ground.

"Oh, that helps a lot," said Rasta. "What did Maximus Mole mean by that?"

"I don't know," said Mo, "but I'll try to find out. I bet Merrymouse might know; I'll go and find her." Off he went, leaving Rasta no happier at all, as he wished he had never tripped over in the first place.

Mo remembered what his dad had said, and he felt he had a mission. He took matters seriously when he thought he could be useful. He scampered on down the hedge side until he caught sight of movement and shouted, "Hey, Merrymouse, come out, come out, wherever you are."

"You know I'm here," said Merrymouse. "Stop being so noisy, and what do you want?"

"Er, sorry, Merrymouse. I just thought you might be able to help me, but if it's too much trouble, I'll ask someone else," said Mo.

Merrymouse liked to feel important, and because she was so very nosy, she wasn't about to let the chance of learning a new titbit go. "Of course I'll help you, Mo. I am always ready to help whenever I can."

"Well," said Mo, and he went on to explain what Rasta had said.

Merrymouse said, "Oh, that's not good; that's not good at all." And she set off along a branch.

"Wait!" shouted Mo. "You haven't helped at all. I won't tell you anything ever again if you aren't going to tell me what you know."

Merrymouse was in a big rush to go spread the gossip, but she stopped to tell Mo about the squirrels.

"When the squirrels get in a huddle in the trees, it means there is something afoot, and they are having an important meeting," said Merrymouse. "Ask your dad about the Squirrel Squad; he will be able to tell you better than me." With that, Merrymouse skittered away as fast as her little legs would carry her—and while she could still remember all the gossip she was very keen to tell.

Mo went home and quickly found Henry Hedgehog sitting on a big, fat dock leaf, rubbing his leg. "Got a nettle sting," said Henry.

Mo sidled up to him and sat down quietly. Henry knew straight away that something was up and said, "OK, Mo, tell me what the matter is." So Mo told him all that he had heard.

"Well, Mo, that certainly needs looking into," he said, and he just sat staring into space.

"What does that mean, Dad?" said Mo.

"OK, son, I'll tell you about the squirrels."

They sat talking for much of the afternoon, and Eenie, Meenie, and Miney joined them. The sun was going down by the time they had finished.

Henry had made the story a lot longer than it needed to be because it was not often he had the full attention of all his little hedgehogs; and he loved it. In short, what he told them was that the squirrels had formed their squad when bad times had been on the island in the past. Some human beings had decided to build some of their big ugly buildings in places that the little folk loved and lived. The squirrels set to work to make sure that the human beings decided that perhaps it was not a good place to do any building after all.

"Wow, how did they manage that?" asked Meenie.

"I think some of them pretended to be ghosts and scared the human beings. They are very scared of ghosts," said Henry.

"I think that was a brilliant idea. Even if the squirrels keep to themselves, it would be good to know that they might help if something is going on," said Hettie.

Eenie said, "I really think we need to go check it out and maybe talk to the squirrels."

"But if they keep to themselves so much, they may not talk to us," said Meenie.

"What does keeping to themselves mean?" asked Mo.

"It means they do not like to mix with other little folk much; haven't you seen them scurrying back up into the trees whenever they spot something on the ground?"

"I thought that was just because something had scared them," said Mo.

Hettie said, "Now remember, I told you that you should not go anywhere on your own, but if you want to check this out, then I want you all to go together to look after each other."

And that's what they did.

The following day, they all set off late in the afternoon to go up to Slopey Woods.

IN SLOPEY WOODS

They set off in their crocodile-line walk, not quite so jauntily as usual, because they were all a little bit worried about what they were going to find out.

When they reached the edge of the wood, they nearly trod on a snake, who shouted, "Watch out, silly hedgehogs!" as they tumbled over him. Then he said, "I know what you've come for." And he slithered away.

"Well, that was helpful," said Miney, just as a little snail squelched up alongside her and said, "I know what he knows, but it will cost you for me to tell you."

"We will find out for ourselves, thank you very much," said Eenie as she stuck her nose up in the air and set off with a bit more purpose. This made Meenie, Miney, and Mo buck up, and they too walked on, a bit more upright and looking a lot braver.

When they were a little way in, Eenie said, "I think Meenie and I should go farther in the woods on our own because we do not make as much noise."

"That's not fair," said Miney. "We want to know too."

"We will tell you all we know when we get back, but in the meantime, we need you to be our very brave lookouts. Do you think you can do that?" asked Eenie.

Miney and Mo both puffed out their little chests and said together, "You can depend on us." And both of them stood at attention and saluted!

"That was a turn-up for the books," said Meenie.

"Do not say that in front of Mo, because he will need an explanation of 'turning up books.'" And they both fell about laughing.

"Quiet," said Eenie. "I can see some activity in the trees."

As they looked up, all they could see was a sea of little tails hanging down from the lower branches. Some of them were quivering, and some of them were still.

"What does that mean?" asked Meenie.

"They are having one of their meetings; we need to get a bit closer to be able to hear."

They both very, very slowly crept closer.

Suddenly, a little face poked out from behind a tree.

And both Eenie and Meenie froze with fright. "Erm, we do not mean any harm," stuttered Eenie.

"We know that, you daft hedgehog; are all hedgehogs daft?" shouted this face as it looked at the two hedgehogs.

"Pretty much," said another in a slightly deeper voice.

"Come on up; we won't bite," said another squirrel.

"We can't climb up there," said Meenie.

"There's a slopey tree trunk over there, and it will bring you up near us; climb up that," said a squirrel, and he swished his tail and leapt to another branch.

Eenie was better at climbing, so she went a little way up the tree trunk. Sergeant Squirrel came down lower. "I am Sergeant Squirrel," said a deep-voiced squirrel, who stepped forward to introduce himself. "You can only stay if you keep quiet; this is a very important meeting." Then he raised his baton to start the meeting.

Then the squirrels proceeded to rearrange themselves in lines on the branches, and when they were all settled, the meeting began.

"Order, order," said one squirrel, and they all shut up at once.

Gosh! That was good, and it worked so well. I will have to remember those words and use them myself when I get home, thought Eenie, and she practiced shouting, *Order, order,* in her head.

"Fellow squirrels," began Sergeant Squirrel, "we have a problem developing that we must address immediately."

"I wish he would not talk so posh and get on with it," whispered one of the squirrels.

"Shut up there," shouted Sergeant. "It has come to our notice that some renegade badgers are plotting something."

There was shuffling, and a grumbling and a mumbling murmur spread through the squirrel ranks at this news.

"Settle down, now; are you not the Squirrel Elite Squad?" shouted Sergeant. "The SES is the best," he continued.

All the squirrels straightened up and stood at attention.

"It has been reported by various means that they intend to do some sort of raid in Slopey Field and that this raid is likely to happen around April next year."

At that all the squirrels relaxed and looked much less interested, and one of them said, "Oh, that's a long way off—nothing to worry about right now."

Sergeant continued as if no one had spoken. "It is important that we get to know as much information as possible and plan well in advance; if we are not prepared, we cannot hope to defend."

"That's right," said one squirrel, and they all nodded in agreement.

"I am glad I have now finally got your attention, squirrels, because this is going to mean some hard work." There was a loud groan. "And I'm splitting you into units all with different tasks."

"Now then, hedgehogs, I think you have heard all that you need. I will get Silly Squirrel to show you out of the woods. If you want to talk to us again, do not sneak into the woods as you just did; come to the edge, and one of my squirrels will see you and ask you what you want. All you have to do is ask for me, and he will bring you to me. Do you understand?" asked Sergeant.

Both Eenie and Meenie nodded in agreement. "We do, Sergeant."

"Now go," said Sergeant. And off they went.

All the hedgehogs set off back home feeling very worried. When they arrived home, they told Henry and Hettie what they had heard.

"Right, that's it," said Henry. "I shall go up to have a word with Sergeant Squirrel tomorrow, and we shall arrange to have a Slopey Field general meeting the day after."

All the little hedgehogs became just a little bit afraid because they had never heard their dad talk like this.

"Don't worry," said Hettie. "Your dad knows what he is doing. Now let's get you all to bed."

"Well," said Mo, "Drake the Duck knows something. I'll go and have a word with him tomorrow."

**Eenie and Meenie meet Silly Squirrel in Slopey Woods,
and they are shocked to see lots of squirrel tails hanging down.**

IX

RUMOURS

Over the next few days, Mo went down to the beck and kept on nagging Drake the Duck about his secret news. Eventually, Drake decided he really ought to tell someone, and it might as well be Mo.

"Well, a few days ago," said Drake, "someone—and I am not telling you who—overheard a conversation that some of the Badger Bankers were having. They are getting very greedy and want to collect as many things as they can. It is not those good badgers, the Brockies, but a few renegades."

"What are renegades?" asked Mo.

"You don't know much, do you, Mo? Renegades are a bunch of folk who split away from others and get together to get up to no good," said Drake.

"Oh, is that all? Some of the badgers have always been greedy anyway; that is nothing new," said Mo disappointedly. He had hoped for some juicy gossip, and all he got was old stuff. So he left Drake and Oscar, who had not bothered to come back up from under the water anyway to keep the conversation going. He went off up Slopey Field to have another nap with his family.

"Any news?" asked Miney when Mo came back.

"No, nothing new, and even if there was, I don't see why I should tell you. You never go out to find out anything anyway and tell me," said Mo as he rolled up into a ball.

DRAKE SPREADS THE WORD
Drake the Duck was quite put out by the rumours, and he even mentioned it again to Oscar the Otter. Oscar got all fired up with this. Serena the Swan glided into the beck just as Drake and Oscar were talking, and Drake began to blush.

Oscar said, "Drake, you are blushing; step behind me so she cannot see you blushing."

"Thank you," said Drake.

Then they told Serena what they had heard, and she said she would do some beaky peeking and swam off.

SERENA SPREADS THE WORD
Serena swam as fast as she could back into the Big River and up to Lake Lynn. She met some water voles on the way and told them about it. They said they had not heard anything but would try to get to know whatever they could. She met some frogs and they said the same.

When she had told as many little folk as she could, she decided it would be easier to fly back to the Rangsey River to get an update, so that is what she did the next day.

MEANWHILE...
Sammy the Grass Snake slithered up to Drake the Duck and hinted that he might know something about what the badgers were planning.

"What?" shouted Drake.

"If you are going to shout at me, I shall not tell you," said Sammy.

"All right, Sammy, but it is important. Please, will you tell me what you know?"

"I heard two of them talking the other day, and they said something about rainbows. But I didn't hear much more as they trundled away."

"Couldn't you have followed them?" shouted Drake.

"You are shouting again, Drake. I am going," said Sammy, and he slithered away.

MEANWHILE...

Eenie and Miney set off on a dawdling trip wandering down Slopey Field, while Merrymouse skittered along in the hedge trying to keep up with them.

Miney was getting annoyed at Merrymouse and told her to go off on one of her own trips. Merrymouse was a bit put out, but she didn't give in easily. She said, "I know something you don't know."

Miney really liked Merrymouse, even though she annoyed her, so she went along with her game.

"Oh yes?" she said. "And what can you possibly know that I don't know?"

"Well," said Merrymouse happily, "I've heard something."

"OK, Merrymouse, I give in. Tell me what you've heard, and I'll let you come on our trip."

"It's the badgers—I heard that they want to get rich; they call it a 'get-rich scheme,' whatever that is."

"Hmm," said Miney. "I think we'll have to think about that. Did you hear anything else?"

"Well," said Merrymouse, spinning out her tail. "One of them said he had a plan, and it had to be very secret."

"Oh," said Eenie and Miney together.

"That alters everything," said Miney.

"In what way does it alter everything?" asked Merrymouse.

"I don't know yet, but when I know, I'll let you know. Then you will know."

Merrymouse pulled a very mousey face. By this time, she was getting very confused, and she was beginning to think she should go off on one of her own trips anyway. So she scurried off on a hazelnut twig.

MEANWHILE...

Meenie and Mo got to the field at the top next to Slopey Woods in the hope of seeing Rasta Rabbit. Rasta was not usually around late mornings, but today he was. Meenie and Mo told Rasta some of what they had heard.

"That's really not cool," said Rasta.

"Well, we know that, Rasta, but we wondered if you had heard anything," said Meenie.

"I haven't, but I will get all the rabbits together today and get them to listen out."

"Thank you, Rasta," said Mo.

"Cool," said Rasta.

TWO DAYS LATER

Dooley too had been hearing some strange things, and he was getting a bit worried. *Something is amiss*, he thought. *I had better go see Henry Hedgehog.*

"Good morning, Dooley," said Henry. "It is nice to see you again. Perhaps you can help us; we are in a bit of a quandary."

"A what?" asked Dooley.

"Oh, sorry, Dooley I mean a bit of a pickle."

"Eh?" said Dooley.

"Oh dear, I am not being very clear, am I?" said Henry. "We have heard some rumours that are not very nice."

"Ah," said Dooley. "I wondered if you had heard."

Henry sat up sharply when Dooley said this and thought, *Does this mean the rumours are true?*

Henry tried to look calm and said, "Tell me what you know Dooley."

And Dooley went on to tell Henry about it.

"Something is happening with some of the badgers, and a few of them are having secret meetings. They are whispering a lot, and they are behaving in a funny way. They are bad tempered if any other badgers go near them and—"

"Whoa," said Henry, "slow down."

"I am sorry, Henry, I am getting very worried by what they might be up to. That is why I came to see you. What can we do?"

"Dooley, we are going to have a Slopey Field general meeting. You have always been our friend, and you are very welcome to come," Said Henry.

Henry meets with Sergeant Squirrel.

X

HENRY MEETS SERGEANT SQUIRREL

Henry set off the following day to see Sergeant Squirrel. He already knew the procedure for speaking with him and he marched to the edge of the woods and waited for Silly Squirrel to show himself.

"Can I have a word with Sergeant, please?" said Henry.

"This way. He is expecting you," said Silly Squirrel.

Henry and Sergeant Squirrel sat down to have a talk, and they were still at it three hours later. They decided this was a serious matter and agreed that a general Slopey Field meeting was called for. Henry agreed to chair the meeting, but Sergeant Squirrel would deal with the main plans and procedures.

Henry and Sergeant Squirrel shook paws, and Silly Squirrel escorted Henry to the edge of the woods.

When Henry arrived home, he had a little talk with Hettie, and then they gathered all the hedgehogs together.

"It has been agreed," said Henry. "We are going to have a general meeting in Slopey Field in two days' time in the afternoon. That will give you all enough time to tell everyone."

"Oh gosh, it does sound serious," said Eenie. "We will have to be very careful to make sure the badgers don't hear about this meeting."

Henry said, "I have already told Dooley that he can come; he is a good badger and will probably be able to help us."

"Right then, all of you listen very carefully," said Hettie "We do not want any of you going anywhere on your own. You must only speak of a meeting, not about anything you have heard, and you must remember who tells you they will be coming. Is that understood?"

"Yes, Mum," said all the hedgehogs at the same time.

That night, the hedgehogs did not sleep very well, and even Eenie said something about "counting sheep," which Mo definitely did not understand. *Who wants to count sheep?* he thought, and then he fell asleep.

The following day all the little hedgehogs set off to tell as many little folk as they could. They saw Rasta first, and he went to tell all his rabbit friends. Then they spied Heath the Hare, and he set off to tell all his hare friends. Merrymouse just watched all that was going, on as usual.

Maximus Mole was quite put out to be one of the last to find out, but as Miney said, "You are always underground during the day, so how can we tell you?"

Meenie said, "You know you are important, Maximus, and we need you at the meeting. Can you come out during the day for this meeting, please?"

"Of course I can," said Maximus Mole, feeling quite proud that Meenie had said he was important.

All the hedgehogs arrived at the beck together. Oscar splashed them, as usual, and they shouted at him, as usual.

"What do you all want?" Oscar said as he swam away without waiting for a reply.

Drake saw them, and they all started talking at once.

"Stop all talking together," said Drake. "I cannot understand anything you are saying."

Oscar was swimming back by this time because he thought he might be missing something.

"Oh," said Oscar, "Well, we are very pleased about this meeting because we have heard lots of things."

Eenie said, "If you tell everyone what you hear at the meeting, then it doesn't have to be repeated."

"That makes sense," said Drake. "Does Serena Swan know about the meeting?"

"No, not yet," said Miney. "We shall have to ask Lilly Lapwing to fly around and see if she can see her."

And so they did.

The afternoon of the meeting arrived. Eenie, Meenie, Miney, and Mo were on their best behaviour, which was very unusual, but they knew this was important.

There were lots of rabbits, hares, some water voles, some sparrows, and two kingfishers. Lilly Lapwing and Jenny Wren had brought some other friends, and Maximus Mole arrived, sending soil in every direction, some hitting Meenie in the eye. Lilly Lapwing shouted, "Stick a poultice on it." And so Jenny Wren did just that. Dooley arrived just in time, for a change. Oscar and Drake arrived with some more ducks, and Serena finally arrived, making Drake blush again.

Miney laughed and said, "If Drake keeps on blushing, he is going to finish up looking like one of those pink birds on long, skinny legs."

"You mean flamingos," said Eenie.

"I know what they are called," grumbled Miney, even though she did not really know.

"Oh, wow!" said Meenie, and they all looked up to see loads of squirrels marching towards them. The Squirrel Squad had arrived. It was a sight to behold. None of the little folk had ever seen them out of the trees. As they marched, all their tails swished from side to side all at the same time.

Oh, it really was going to be a big meeting.

"Order, order," shouted Henry.

And everyone in the field went quiet.

"Harrumph," said Henry clearing his throat. "I have been asked to be in charge of this meeting because there are some rumours and concerns about what some badgers may or may not be up to," said Henry.

Then everyone started talking all at once.

"Order, order," shouted Henry again. "You will all have a chance to speak. But we all need to know what you have heard, so you will have to take it in turns."

Eventually they all went quiet, and very slowly, each of the main little folk took it in turns to tell all of the rumours that he or she had heard.

"Well," said Henry, scratching his chin, "it appears we may have something to worry about. What do you think, Sergeant Squirrel?"

"I think we should all split into groups to find out more and arrange another meeting to discuss what we have learned. Then we can decide on a strategy," said Sergeant Squirrel.

"What's a strategy?" asked Mo.

"Shut up, Mo, and listen," said Meenie.

"We should try to spy on the badgers," said Maximus Mole.

"That is a very good idea, Maximus," said Sergeant Squirrel.

"I can help," squeaked Merrymouse, but no one heard her.

"Dooley, can you do any spying?" asked Henry.

"I can try," said Dooley. "They do not tend to notice me when I'm around, so I might be able to get to know something."

"I can help," squeaked Merrymouse, but no one heard her again.

The water voles said that they could get near the tower by the river and might be able to hear something.

"Good, good," said Sergeant Squirrel.

"Oscar, I'm afraid you make too much noise. They would hear you, so I am sorry, but you can't help."

"Oh, all right," said Oscar, not the least bit bothered because it sounded like hard work.

"I can help," squeaked Merrymouse, but no one heard her again.

Heath the Hare said he would do some scouting, and the squirrels said they would post a small squad in the Little Oak Tree at the bottom of Midgley's field.

"Right, that sounds like a plan," said Sergeant.

"I can help," squeaked Merrymouse, and this time they heard her.

All the little folk turned to look at Merrymouse.

"Oh," said Merrymouse, surprised, and she ducked down out of sight.

"Come out, Merrymouse, so we can listen to you," said Hettie. And very slowly, the leaves rustled, and one slightly scared eye appeared, blinked once, and ducked out of sight again.

"Come on, Merrymouse, we haven't got all day," said Eenie. Slowly, the leaves parted, and Merrymouse moved about to get comfortable.

"What do you think you can do, Merrymouse?" asked Sergeant Squirrel.

"I am very small, and often little folks don't see me. I might be able to get close enough to them to hear what they are saying," said Merrymouse.

"Bravo," shouted Mo. "That's a brilliant idea."

"But," said Henry, "I do not think you should go on your own; Meenie, will you go with her?"

"Of course I will," said Meenie bravely, not feeling the least bit brave.

Merrymouse nervously peeking out of the hedge.

XI

SPYING

Dooley had no idea how he was going to find out anything. But he had promised his friends, so he was going to do his very best. When dusk arrived, he went to High Tower.

Bundle, one of the resident badgers, said, "To what do we owe the honour of this visit, Dooley? You don't come very often. Are you going to come to stay in High Tower?"

"Er, no, I just thought it would be nice to come and see how everyone is doing. It was because of my wish that the Wishing Wizard gave us the High Tower, and I thought I should come now and then. Is that all right?" asked Dooley.

"Oh yes, Dooley, we really like it here. Everything is great, no wind or rain or soggy paws. Are you sure you don't want to come and join us?"

"I quite like my sett," said Dooley, "but I might change my mind, if that would be all right?"

"Of course, Dooley, you are always welcome."

One of the other badgers, Bosco, was scowling at Bundle, and as soon as Dooley left, he marched over to Bundle.

"What on earth are you thinking about, Bundle?" he asked. "We don't want anyone else moving in. What about all our plans?"

"Oh sorry, Bosco, but we can't be rude to Dooley, can we? After all it was Dooley who got us High Tower."

Dooley realised that they were whispering. Then he thought he should get friendly with Bundle, and maybe he would tell him what he wanted to know.

When he had a chance, he went over, sat next to Bundle, and said, "You are such a good badger, Bundle. You make me feel very welcome."

Bundle said, "We can't do anything else, can we? Because we wouldn't have all this luck if it wasn't for you."

"What luck is that, Bundle?"

"Well High Tower and our plans."

"Ah, the plans."

"Oh, you know about the plans?" asked Bundle with a look of relief on his face.

"I heard, Bundle. Not bad, eh?" said Dooley, and he held his breath, hoping that Bundle would tell him something.

"I think they are brilliant, and if we do get rich, then Bosco says we shall all be very happy," said Bundle.

Now what does that mean? thought Dooley.

"True, Bundle, but it won't be very easy," said Dooley, scratching his chin.

"Bosco says if we plan it for April next year, there should be plenty of them around."

"Plenty of—" Then Dooley shut up because Bosco was coming back really rather quickly.

"Hello, Bosco! I am pleased I came along to see you, and Bundle has told me how wonderful High Tower is. I think I'll get going now, though, because I have some rummaging to do," he said as he jumped up to leave.

Bosco said, "You are very welcome, Dooley." And he turned to scowl at Bundle.

Dooley heard Bosco ask Bundle if he had told him anything about their plan, and Bundle said no.

Thank goodness, thought Dooley as he left High Tower.

MEANWHILE...

Heath the Hare was also wondering how on earth he could get to know what the badgers were up to. He took off back to the moors near Midgley's farm for a big hare ponder.

"Right, that's what I'll do," he said out loud a little later, as he scurried, rather fast even for a hare, down to the beck.

He shouted, "Oscar, are you about?" Then water cascaded all over Heath.

"Oh, Oscar, why do you always have to wet everyone?"

"Because that's what I'm good at," said Oscar.

"Well, how about trying to be good at something else then?" asked Heath.

"All right, I give in. What do you want?" asked Oscar.

"I have to try to find out something about the badgers' plans, and I could use your help," said Heath.

"So long as it is not hard work," said Oscar "What do you have in mind?"

"I need to go to High Tower and find out anything I can about what the *bad badgers* are planning. Have you any ideas?"

"You need to be there at dusk, just about when the tower appears, and wait to see who comes out. I know that Bosco Badger is not a good badger, so if you see him, it would be best to follow him and try to hear something that is said," said Oscar.

"Oh thank you, Oscar. Hares are not very good at keeping quiet because we don't know how to move very slowly, but I shall try."

MEANWHILE...

**Merrymouse edges around a toadstool
to watch the badgers meeting.**

Merrymouse was feeling very happy that she had been given an important job to do. She was also determined to prove to all the little folk that she was not just a dizzy little dormouse. She knew she had a long way to travel for a little mouse, and she was glad that Meenie was coming with her. They decided they would get as close as she could during the day to where the badgers tended to forage and then settle down to wait for them to come out at night. They also knew that it would mean staying out all night, because it would be difficult to see well enough to get back home. When Merrymouse thought about it all, she started to get very worried. Meenie started telling daft jokes to keep her mind off it until she told him his jokes were not funny.

They set off late that afternoon down the hedge of Slopey Field and then along River Rangsey's bank to the big bridge. This made them quite frightened because cars came over the bridge very fast. They had to keep as close to the outer edge as possible and tried to look invisible.

When they reached the other side they crouched down, huffing and puffing, and Merrymouse's little heart was beating very, very fast.

Now, she thought, *I have to decide where is the best place to wait and hide.*

They crept as close as they could to where High Tower usually appeared and snuggled down in some long grass to wait, and then they fell asleep. All of a sudden, they heard some funny noises and looked up. *Oh, golly gosh! The badgers are moving about; I hope they don't see us,* thought Meenie.

The badgers gathered in a huddle, and Merrymouse, who made less noise than Meenie, crept as close as she dared to try to listen. There was a full moon and a clear sky, and she could see them talking.

"Now then, Bradley and Brindle, are we all in agreement? More importantly, have we all done our research?" asked Bundle.

"I'll take it from here," growled Bosco, and he started to draw a map in the soil in front of them all.

"This," he said, "is Slopey Field. Now, we all know that lots of rainbows come out in April in Slopey Field, so it is decided that is where and when we shall do our digging."

"But we shall need to decide on where we shall enter the field," he added.

"I reckon near Midgley's gate, where we can all get under the bottom fence," said Bundle.

"All right, that sounds good, but when shall we plan to do this?" asked Bradley.

"Well, I think we shall only get two chances to do this before the little folk cotton on to what we are doing. I think we should post a lookout to spot a rainbow. Then a message is sent to us, and we move as quickly as we can. We have to move as quickly as we can because rainbows can disappear," said Bosco.

"If it fails the first time, then we can take the very next opportunity and try the same thing again," said Bundle.

"Also, it is over six months away before we do this, so we had better plan another meeting in March to get all the details right," said Brindle.

"OK, that's it then. We shall meet again on the first moon of March, and don't be late," ordered Bosco as they all trundled away.

"Oh," said Merrymouse out loud, and then she worried that they might have heard her. Luckily, they did not hear her. She was very scared by what she had heard and did not really understand it.

I hope this helps the other little folk, she thought as she snuggled down even farther to try to sleep.

Bradley, Brindle, Bundle, and Bosco hatching their plans.

XII

SECOND GENERAL MEETING

All the little folk were getting quite excited and scared in equal doses by all that was happening. Sergeant Squirrel knew they had to calm everyone down and get their master plan as clear as possible.

The day of the next meeting arrived. This time there were even more little folk attending.

"Welcome to you all," said Henry in his loudest voice.

"Yes, indeed," said Sergeant Squirrel, even louder.

"Silly Squirrel, can you take all the newcomers into a corner and update them on all that has happened, please?" asked Sergeant Squirrel.

"Of course," said Silly Squirrel. "Everyone who is new to the meeting, follow me, please," he said, puffing his little chest out and feeling very important.

Drake the Duck noticed that Serena had arrived, and he made sure he was sitting as close to her as he could get.

"Order, order," said Henry again, even louder.

"At our last meeting, three of you went on missions to try to learn more about what the badgers were planning," said Henry. "So let's start with you, Dooley. What have you got to report?"

"I went up into High Tower," said Dooley, "and I was met by Bundle Badger. He made me very welcome, but Bosco Badger was watching us all the time, which I found a bit strange. Bundle was very grateful for High Tower, and he told me they only had it because of me."

"Yes, yes, hurry up, Dooley. What did he tell you?" asked Silly Squirrel.

"Don't interrupt, Silly," ordered Sergeant Squirrel. "Let him tell it in his own time; that way he will not miss anything."

"Sorry, Sergeant," said Silly, hanging his head and trying to hide behind his tail.

Dooley continued. "And these are Bundle's actual words: 'I think they are great, and if we get rich, then as Bosco says, we shall all be very happy.' I didn't know what he meant, but I pretended I did and told him it would not be easy. Then Bundle said, 'Bosco says if we plan it for April next year, there should be plenty of them around.' Then Bosco came hurrying across the room, and Bundle stopped talking."

Dooley stopped talking, and everyone just stared at each other.

"Right," said Henry. "I think we should hear from both Heath and Merrymouse first before we try to work out what this all means."

"Good, good," said Sergeant Squirrel. "Heath Hare, are you ready?"

Heath the Hare stood up very proudly, cleared his throat, and in his very deep voice started to tell them what he knew.

"I ran to High Tower and waited until some badgers came out. After a few minutes, a few went out together, and they were talking to each other. I thought it best to follow them. They stopped to forage around a bit, and then one of them laughed and said, 'We might not have to do much of this if we find the gold. Bosco says we will be rich, and I know that if you are rich, you get other folks to work for you. That's what all the human beings do.'"

Heath went on, "I did not understand what they meant, but it did not sound good. Just as I was thinking about what they said, one of them looked in my direction. I was sure he'd seen me, so I pretended to be doing some searching and foraging of my own. As soon as I could, I ran away."

"Now, that is interesting. I think when we have heard what Merrymouse and Meenie have learned, perhaps we shall have a clearer picture or even know what they are planning. Go ahead, Merrymouse; tell us what you found out," said Sergeant Squirrel.

Merrymouse was very, very nervous, and she started twitching her tail. When she started to speak, she was even stuttering.

"Calm down, Merrymouse," whispered Meenie. "We all think you are the bravest little mouse ever."

This really made Merrymouse feel very proud. She stood on her back legs as tall as she could, which wasn't very tall anyway, and told them her tale.

When she told them about scurrying over the bridge, they all said "Ooooh," with a little bit of fear. Merrymouse had really been a very brave mouse indeed.

She told them that after they had settled down to wait, which seemed like ages, some of the badgers came out. She crept a little nearer to hear them. The moon was good, and they huddled down and began to talk.

"Come on, come on. You are keeping us in suspense," said Miney.

"Shut up, Miney, this is important," said Eenie.

"Bosco, Bundle, Bradley, and Brindle were the badgers," said Merrymouse, continuing her story. "They talked about research, and then Bosco started to draw a map in the soil. It was a map of Slopey Field."

At this, there was another big "ooooh" from all the little folk as they crept a bit nearer to Merrymouse so that they would not miss anything.

Merrymouse took a big gulp of air, because she now began to realise just how important her story was.

"Bosco said something about lots of rainbows in Slopey Field in April," said Merrymouse, "and then he said so that is where and when they would do their digging."

There was yet another big "ooooh" from all the little folk.

"Then," continued Merrymouse, "he said they needed to decide where they would come into Slopey Field and Bundle said near Midgley's gate because they could get under the fence there."

There was another even bigger "ooooh" from everyone.

Merrymouse was beginning to get a bit upset now because she had never had all this attention, and Mo nudged her and winked, trying to encourage her.

"Well," she continued, "one of the badgers said they would only have two chances to do it, so if the first rainbow disappeared too quickly, they could try again. He said they would post a look-out, to send a message, as soon as a rainbow appeared. That's it, really," said Merrymouse as she sank to the floor, quite worn out, and tried to make herself as invisible as she could.

"Good stuff, Merrymouse. You have both been very brave, and you have found out some important information," said Sergeant Squirrel.

At this, the little hedgehogs started to clap.

"Stop the clapping," said Henry. "Merrymouse and Meenie have done well, but this is a very serious matter. Would you like to continue the meeting now, Sergeant?"

"Oh, I nearly forgot," said Merrymouse. "They said they would have another meeting on the first day of March."

Some of the little folk started to leave because they thought there was no urgency; it was such a long time before March would be here.

"Please sit back down, all of you. It is important that we formulate—sorry—make plans now so we know how to deal with this problem," Sergeant Squirrel was always using big words whenever he had the chance.

"First, do we know what the badgers are up to?"

There was silence.

"I think—" said Dooley, and they all let out a big sigh. Dooley ignored them and said, "I think it could be something to do with the gold at the end of a rainbow."

Now this really took everyone's breath away. There was a bigger silence, then some shuffling, and then everyone started to talk at once.

"Order, order," said Sergeant Squirrel, who was getting quite fed up of saying it.

"Isn't it just a story about a pot of gold being at the end of a rainbow?" asked Meenie.

"Yes," said Eenie. "It is a legend, but who is to say whether a legend is definitely true or not true? The badgers obviously believe it is true."

"If it is true," said Miney, "then we shall have to stop them, because legends are important, and we do not want them digging up our field."

"Why are they doing this, do you think, Dooley?" asked Meenie.

"Because they are greedy, and they think it will make them rich," he replied.

"How silly," said Silly Squirrel.

"OK, OK," said Sergeant Squirrel, "I think we are all agreed we have to stop them. Now we have to make our own plans. I know it is a long time off, but we need to get some plans sorted before winter sets in and before the hedgehogs' hibernation time. So I suggest we take time to think hard about this."

And they all sat quietly thinking.

"Now you've had a little time to think we need to designate—sorry, decide on groups of little folk who can take action."

Serena Swan spoke for the first time and told them that she knew of some rats in Big Town who had access to some things they might be able to use against the badgers. There was a big toy factory, and sometimes they threw big boxes of toys away. Some of these could be used to help.

"I know they have boxes of toys that shoot Ping-Pong balls; perhaps we could use them to stop the badgers," she said.

"Well, it is worth a try," said Sergeant Squirrel. "Can you contact them?"

"I shall, but we shall have to arrange to get them over here to Slopey Field."

"I'll help," shouted Drake, standing up way too quickly. Serena looked at him thankfully. Drake, of course, blushed.

"I can help as well," said Oscar, "We can bring them over the river on something that floats, but we will need a bit more help than just Serena, Drake, and me."

"I can bring some of my friends," said Serena. "We can fly down at the end of February and swim over with Drake and Oscar to bring them back."

"Right," said Sergeant Squirrel. "Then that is Plan A, but we also need a Plan B in case Plan A doesn't work."

Now they all had another think for a long time and were beginning to struggle for ideas until Hettie decided she should say something.

"I believe that if you try and wish and hope and concentrate hard enough, you can make your dreams come true," she said.

"Hettie is right; we cannot give up. We all feel the same, and if we all try and wish and hope, we can make something special happen," said Henry.

"If we all wish and hope and concentrate and surround the end of the rainbow and try to put as much love and hope and caring into it as possible, I believe that dreams can come true," said Hettie.

And all the little folk looked at each other and started nodding, and they were so full of joy.

"Well done; that's sorted that out then," said Sergeant Squirrel, bringing them all to attention. "Then that is our Plan B, but we must plan it in detail."

Eenie, Meenie, Miney, and Mo were all getting quite confused by now.

"The squirrels will set up a watch in the small oak tree at the bottom of Midgley's field," said Sergeant Squirrel.

"I'll get lots of my rabbit friends sitting in the grass near the fence," said Rasta.

"I'll keep watch from the beck," said Oscar.

"So will I," said Drake.

"We shall be with you too," said Serena.

Heath said, in his deep voice, "A lot of my friends will be on standby, ready to run around and spread the word if Plan B is to be put into action."

Lilly Lapwing said she, Jenny Wren, and some of her friends would watch things from the air.

Merrymouse said she would watch from the hedge.

Maximus Mole said he would be ready to charge around the under field to spread the word, and he would build more tunnels in readiness.

The hedgehogs said they would be on standby, ready to form the circle when told.

"Good work, little folk," said Sergeant Squirrel, "We have Plan B."

"We shall have another meeting on the first day of March to finalise the plans. Have a good winter, everyone," he shouted.

And all the squirrels formed lines and marched back up to Slopey Woods.

XIII

TIME TO SLEEP

As autumn slowly became winter, life in Rangseysdale for the little folk became much quieter. The rabbits came out quite regularly to search for food, but they did not stay out for long, because it was very cold. Heath the Hare and his friends did not really stop doing anything because they were always active and foraging for food. Merrymouse ate food she had stored, and she curled up and slept a lot. The squirrels stayed in the trees and ate the nuts they had managed to get back from the good badgers, as well as those they had stored themselves.

Oscar was a bit put out when the beck started to freeze over and he could not do any splish-splashing, but he loved to slide all over the ice. Drake did not much like the cold, but he was quite happy that it meant he did not get quite so wet and muddy. When the snow came down, even the badgers were reluctant to come out.

Maximus Mole only trundled about now and then, as the ground was so hard, but he managed to dig some tunnels lower down. He was quite put out when the snow came down, because lots of human beings came into Slopey Field. He could not understand why they walked all the way to the top of the field, pulling some odd things, and then they slid all the way to the bottom. Then they did it all again. He decided human beings were really silly.

The hedgehogs had all bedded down in their little secret places and rolled up into prickly balls to go to sleep for the winter. Henry, however, knew how important it was to be ready for the badgers in April, so he asked Sergeant Squirrel to make sure they were all woken up in time for their first meeting in March.

Slowly, winter started to thaw into spring, and little snow-drops were poking their heads out of the ground. Then crocus joined the snowdrops, and lots of pretty colours started to show on the ground. The hedgehogs would be waking when the daffodils joined this throng.

"Stand to," shouted a voice.

Oh, what on earth is that noise? thought Hettie, yawning.

"Henry, can you hear me?" said the voice again.

Henry unrolled himself and groggily grunted, "Yes."

"It's time to get up; time to get up," said Sergeant Squirrel.

Oh dear, I wish he was not so loud, thought Henry, wanting nothing more than to stay snuggled up in all his dry leaves.

"OK, Sergeant Squirrel. We are waking up; thank you," said Henry, pulling a very grumpy face.

Slowly, all the hedgehogs started to wake up and unroll. They pushed one leg out and then another, rubbed their noses and paws, and grunted a lot. When they tried to stand, it was not always successful, because their legs were very wobbly, and they rolled over again. When they had all finally woken up and remembered about the badgers, they were very quiet, thinking.

"Come on, all of you, liven up. We have work to do," said Henry.

All the hedgehogs groaned, and Hettie soothingly said, "Come on, now; where are all those lovely, clever hedgehogs that were so helpful with our plans in October?" said Hettie.

Eenie, Meenie, and Miney sat up straight; Mo tried to sit up straight but toppled over.

"Good, now that we've got your attention, the first thing we do is have something to eat," said Henry.

Food was the magic word. They scurried and lunged for all the food they could find and then gobbled it up as fast as they could.

Things were back to normal in the hedgehog camp.

On the first day of March, Slopey Field was buzzing with little folk.

XIV

THE BIG MEETING

All the little folk were drifting in to Slopey Field from every direction. Eenie, Meenie, Miney, and Mo had done a very good job of spreading the word. Henry felt very proud of them.

Sergeant Squirrel had led his squad members down from Slopey Woods, and he was holding court with them gathered all around him.

Sergeant Squirrel said, "Now, squirrels, this is probably going to be the most important thing that you ever do. We have to protect the rainbow gold. It is a legend that cannot be changed. We are sworn to protect it, and that is what we shall do." He puffed out his chest. All the squirrels followed suit; it was a very funny sight.

Henry greeted Sergeant Squirrel, and they sat together waiting for some sort of order to appear in Slopey Field.

The rabbits tumbled over each other while trying to look for a place to sit, and Maximus Mole was getting quite annoyed because they kept getting in his way. Maximus was really quite small, and he couldn't see everything that was happening. Eenie, Meenie, Miney, and Mo sat in a line next to Hettie. Heath the Hare sat next to them, and Oscar the Otter lolloped to sit beside him. Drake the Duck and Maximus had managed to get to the front next to Merrymouse, Lilly

Lapwing, and Jenny Wren. Dooley arrived just in time but sat at the back because he felt a bit sorry. He thought it was because of him that the Wishing Wizard had given the badgers High Tower. The *bad badgers* would not have had such big ideas about stealing gold if it were not for that. So he thought it was all his fault. Henry saw him and guessed what he was thinking. He said, "Come on, Dooley, sit with us. You are a good badger and a good friend."

So Dooley moved to the front and felt so much better. He smiled for the first time since before winter had set in. Very slowly, all the little folk began to settle down to listen.

Sergeant Squirrel looked around and banged his baton on a stone. "Order, order," he shouted. Everyone stopped talking and waggling about and settled down. Hundreds of little faces looked at Sergeant Squirrel and Henry.

Henry cleared his throat and said, "Harrumph." Then he stood up to address all the little folk. "I think we all know why we are here today, but to make sure you all do, I will tell you that it has come to our attention that some renegade *bad badger* bankers are planning to steal the gold from the end of the rainbow very soon."

All the eyes of the little folk got wider and wider, and they were very worried.

"But," Henry went on, "we are not going to let this happen." A muffled cheer went up. "We have two plans to stop this happening, and Sergeant Squirrel is going to explain these to you."

"Yes, right," said Sergeant Squirrel, standing up. "At the end of last year, we had a meeting after we had managed to get as much information as possible about what the *bad badgers* were intending to do. We have to thank Eenie, Meenie, Miney, Mo, Drake the Duck, Jenny Wren, and Lilly Lapwing for information, and we have to thank Dooley, Heath Hare, Meenie, and, last but not least, Merrymouse for carrying out secret missions."

All the little folk shouted, "Thank you!" almost at the same time but not quite, which made an awful noise.

"Who are the *bad badgers?*" asked one little field mouse.

"We know they are Bosco, Bundle, Bradley, and Brindle, and they have been having meetings and doing some planning," said Henry. At this, all the little folk looked worriedly at each other.

"Right," Sergeant Squirrel went on. "We know their plans, so we can be prepared. That is very important. I am going to put forward details of the plans we have already discussed, and if any of you want to ask anything or offer any ideas, we shall talk about them at the end."

Sergeant Squirrel went on to explain Plan A to them, and there was a big noise when he finished because everyone wanted to ask questions.

"One at a time, please," said Henry.

"Yes, be patient," said Heath the Hare, who did not usually speak much because of his very deep, scary voice, but it made them all to shut up.

"Thank you," whispered Henry.

"How are we going to get the pop guns from Big Town?" asked a rabbit.

"Serena Swan has offered her services, along with Oscar the Otter and Drake the Duck," said Sergeant Squirrel.

Serena stepped forward. "I have brought three friends with me who have offered to help," she said; two swans took their place at her side, but it was the third friend that caused the most interest. A lovely little duck came out from behind Serena as she announced, "Sally and Sylvie are my cousins, and this is my best friend, Dyllis Duck."

Drake the Duck blushed whenever he saw Serena, but when he saw Dyllis, his eyes nearly popped out of his head, and he went even redder, nearly like a tomato.

"Oh, Henry, look," said Hettie, "I think Drake is smitten."

And as they all looked, Mo whispered, "Hee hee, I think he's going to change into a flamingo!"

"Shut up, Mo; you will embarrass him," said Eenie.

"Good, good," said Sergeant Squirrel carrying on with the meeting. "Then we shall arrange the finer details. Perhaps the three swans should take one flotilla and Drake, Dyllis, and Oscar the other. What do you think?" he said as he looked at them.

"That seems like a good idea," said Serena. "What do you think, Oscar?"

"How is Drake going to manage since he doesn't like water?" asked Oscar.

Drake was struggling to talk, but he huffed and puffed. Then he stood up straight, puffed his chest out, and said, "I shall manage quite well, thank you, Oscar. This is an important mission."

Dyllis looked at Drake; he managed a small smile, and his blush started to disappear.

"Now," said Henry, "We need to decide when this mission is to start."

Serena said, "We need to go as soon as we can, because I have a friend called Ratty, and he and his friends are willing to help us. They will get the pop guns and Ping Pong balls down to the side of the river for us, and they have managed to get a hold of some little canoes to carry them over. I need to let them know, so I suggest the day after tomorrow if the weather is good. If it isn't, then we go the following day. That will give me time to speak to Ratty."

"The pop guns will have to be hidden until we need them. Any suggestions?" asked Sergeant Squirrel.

Dooley piped up. "There is an old shed at the bottom of the field next to Slopey Field. There is an old badger sett near it. I can store some in the old shed and transfer them into the old sett during the day, when the *bad badgers* are asleep. They don't know about this sett."

"Excellent," said Henry.

There was a bit of a lull while they all tried to take in everything they had heard, and then another rabbit asked, "What is Plan B?"

"Ah," said Sergeant Squirrel, "I think it would be best if Henry explains that to you."

Henry knew that this was probably going to be the most important speech that he would ever have to make, so he stood up as tall as he possibly could to look at everyone.

"We have all had hopes and dreams and great big wishes all our lives, haven't we?" asked Henry.

All the little folk looked at each other and started nodding.

"We all hope for things, though we do not always get what we hope for. Sometimes we get even better things than we had hoped for, and many times we don't realise that we have actually helped our hopes become real because we have helped ourselves to make them come true."

"That's true," said a squirrel as they thought about it, and then they all nodded in agreement.

"So we have our hopes and dreams and wishes, and we help ourselves try to make these come true, don't we?"

"Yes," they all said together.

"Good, then. Now I am ready to tell you about Plan B," said Henry.

PLAN B

"The badgers," said Henry, "have decided to carry out their raid in April because it is the month when most rainbows appear. They have decided it is to be in Slopey Field because they know many rainbows have appeared here before, and they are sure there is gold here. They are going to make two attempts, and we need to be prepared for them. Sergeant Squirrel has organised squads of squirrels to be lookouts so that we can all be warned when the *bad badgers* are coming."

Sergeant Squirrel took over then and said, "One squad is going to be placed in the little oak tree at the bottom of Midgley's field, and the other is to be behind the hedge near where the scarecrow lives. As soon as they see the badgers, they will use our squirrel whistles that we have made out of acorns to tell Lilly Lapwing, Jenny Wren, and their friends to fly over to alert you all. Heath the Hare and his friends along with Maximus Mole will be on standby to help spread the news."

He went on. "Plan A will be set up in advance. The pop guns will be in place, and the squirrels and rabbits will shoot the balls at the badgers. The rabbits will load the guns, and the squirrels have worked out how to pull the triggers."

"If Plan A looks as if it is not working, then the lookout squirrels will whistle again, but this time they will whistle three times, take a breath, and then whistle three more times. That will be the signal to go to Plan B."

"But you still have not told us what Plan B is," said a rabbit.

"When you all hear those whistles, you are to rush to take your places around Slopey Field in a circle around the bottom of the rainbow. You are to hold hands, paws, claws, and wings, and then you are to look at the rainbow and wish and hope as hard as you possibly can for something special to happen to stop the badgers. If all the little folk are wishing and hoping all at the same time, it will be a very big, strong wish," said Henry.

There was a silence. Then there was a shuffle. Then there was a great big cheer.

"Yes, we can do this," they all started saying.

"That was magnificent, Henry," said Hettie with a little tear in her eye.

Serena, Sally, and Sylvie pull one canoe, and
Oscar, Drake, and Dyllis pull the other canoe.

XV

MISSION ACROSS BIG RIVER

Later that day Serena Swan contacted Ratty Rat, and they arranged to meet at the river's edge in Big Town the following day early in the morning, when the *bad badgers* had gone to sleep.

Drake had been talking with Dyllis about the mission, and they were talking so much that Oscar was having difficulty getting a word in. They decided that they would go up the river a little way to where the current was less strong and then swim across to Big Town. Serena joined them, and they discussed all the details and agreed to meet on the river bank upstream, ready to cross to Big Town at dawn on mission day.

"Wake up, Drake," said Oscar, splish-splashing as usual.

"Oh, Oscar, do you have to splash so much?" asked Drake. "I was already awake."

Drake tentatively put his feet into the water. When Dyllis swam to his side, he puffed up and swam so well that he was amazed. They all set off on their big mission.

Big River is really big and wide near the sea, so they swam along the side of the river where it was quite shallow and there were fewer waves. It took them a little longer than they thought, and Drake was beginning to get worried. Serena, Sally, and

Sylvie were waiting for them, and they all set off together to cross Big River.

Drake had never swum so much in his life, and he never dreamed he would cross this river. He was so very proud to be doing this special mission.

When they glided in to the other side, they saw hundreds of rats swarming on the river bank.

"Golly gosh!" said Dyllis, "I hope they are friendly; it is quite scary to see so many little rat folk at once."

"Don't worry, Dyllis," said Serena. "I have known Ratty for a long time; he is a good rat."

All the rats had formed a long line, and they were passing first little pop guns and some pop cones and then little Ping-Pong balls down to each canoe. It did not take long to load the canoes. The rats had managed to fasten three lots of tough string at the front of each canoe so that they could be pulled along. Serena took up the lead string, and Sally and Sylvie took up the other two for one canoe. Drake and Dyllis took up two strings of the other canoe with Oscar taking the lead string. They were off!

They had to swim very carefully because the waves kept sweeping them off course. It took a lot longer to get back to the other side of the river. They ended up downstream, and of course, the river was wider there. Drake was getting a little bit worried, but he dared not show it.

Finally, they managed to land—which is exactly what happened, because the canoe Drake, Dyllis, and Oscar were towing tipped over just as they reached the bank.

Sergeant Squirrel had asked Rasta Rabbit to arrange for all his friends to meet them there, and they managed to save everything from getting wet. Some of the rabbits got very muddy, which they didn't much like, and Rasta was a bit put out because he got his dreadlocks wet.

Now there were so many little folk; it was amazing. They all carried the pop guns, pop cones, and Ping-Pong balls to the shed at the bottom of the field by Slopey Field. They opened some of the boxes to take some to Sergeant Squirrel so that he could decide how to set them up.

Just as they reached Slopey Field, Drake stubbed one of his feet.

"Put a poultice on it!" shouted Oscar.

"Oh no, not now," said Drake, as Lilly Lapwing herself swooped down and stuck a poultice on his foot.

"I am very proud to put the poultice on your foot," said Lilly. "You are a hero duck today."

Dyllis beamed at him with a huge smile. From then on, until the poultice dropped off of course, Drake wore his poultice like a medal. He was so happy.

Now all they had to do was wait. Sergeant Squirrel explained Plan A in detail to all the squirrels and rabbits that were going to carry out this mission and to Maximus Mole, who had offered to play a very important part in this plan. Sergeant Squirrel was not very good at drawing, but he managed to scribble something in the mud. After a lot of talking, groaning, chitchatting, and even laughing, they all managed to understand.

PLAN A STRATEGY

Sergeant Squirrel said, "Maximus Mole is going to build twenty mounds of soil in two rows so that we can set up the pop gobs and pop cones. This can be done well in advance. and the badgers will not notice. There will be a row of ten pop cones in the bottom row and a row of ten pop guns in a row a little way above.

"The top row of guns fires first. On hearing the signal, these will be fired first because they can fire higher and farther. The rabbits are to load the guns. The squirrels are to pull the triggers in twos. There will be a string around the trigger, and the squirrels will either pull hard on each end or tie it to their tails and run together. They are going to practice to find out which is best."

"The bottom row, the cones, fire second. On hearing the second signal, these will be fired. The squirrels are to load the cones as fast as they can. The rabbits are to bash the trigger with both paws or jump on the trigger. They are going to practice to find out which is best."

After they had all agreed and decided when they were going to practice, they all started clapping hands and high-fiving. But while they were practicing, it became obvious there was a problem. The pop guns and cones were very light and kept moving around when the little folk tried to shoot them. "Oh dear," said Henry, "we shall have to have a meeting about this." And he sent a message to Sergeant Squirrel.

XVI

THE END—OR IS IT?

Sergeant and Silly Squirrel sat with Henry and Hettie Hedgehog along with Heath the Hare, Rasta Rabbit, and Drake the Duck—with Dyllis, of course, who was now always at his side. Sergeant Squirrel advised them all that the practicing for Plan A was going very well, and Maximus Mole had built all the mounds to support the pop guns and cones, but there was a problem, which he went on to explain. Eenie, Meenie, Miney, and Mo had come along too, and Mo piped up, "I've got an idea."

They all looked at Mo, and Eenie raised one eyebrow, which flustered Mo because they did not usually listen to him, but he went on. "If two hedgehogs put their backs against the guns at either side, it will keep them from moving around! Look, I'll show you." He promptly got up and shouted at Meenie to help. They both stiffened their bristles and pushed against each side of a pop gun.

"Golly gosh! He's right," said Sergeant Squirrel. "Well done, Mo." They all started clapping their feet and paws.

"Ah, but," said Meenie, to which there was a big groan, "there are lots of pop guns and only us, four hedgehogs."

"We have got lots of friends, silly Meenie," said Mo. "We can get their help."

Eenie said, "Yes," very loudly and clapped her paws. "Right, Miney and I shall go together in one direction, and Meenie and Mo can go in another. We shall round them up." And off they went.

A little while later, Hettie said, "Henry, has there been some rain? It looks like the beck is overflowing." When they looked again, they could see it was not the beck overflowing but a big stream of hedgehogs moving towards them.

Merrymouse squeaked loudly and skittered about the hedge, telling everyone, and Jenny Wren got in on the action.

"Magnificent," said Henry. "We are very proud of you; you have saved the day!" And Eenie, Meenie, Miney, and Mo all wore the proudest grins that stretched from ear to ear.

Now they were ready. A daily lookout squad was posted in the Little Oak Tree at the bottom of Midgley's field, and some rabbits were stationed by the scarecrow. Oscar was keeping a constant vigil down in the beck, and Maximus Mole was on alert at the bottom of the field.

On the third day of April, there were some showers followed by some sunshine, and all the little folk became a bit jumpy because they knew this might come on this day. A rainbow started to appear in Slopey Field.

"Oh no, this could be it," said Eenie. But as she said it, the rainbow started to fade away.

On the fourth day of April, it rained during the night, and then in the early morning, it was fine. Then it started to do the same again, and a brighter rainbow started to appear.

The squirrels were getting very agitated, and their tails were swishing about in the oak tree.

"They are coming," said one, and he blew his whistle as loud as he could.

Everyone went on standby. All the hedgehogs got into position, and the rabbit and squirrel squads staffed their guns and got ready to fire.

There was some scuffling around the bottom fence, and a rabbit near the scarecrow saw a badger and shouted, "They are coming. They are coming!"

The gun squad got ready. The whistle was blown.

As soon as the guns were loaded, Sergeant Squirrel shouted, "Fire!"

"Oh no," growled Bundle, "how did they find out?"
"We can't stop now," ordered Bosco.

The hedgehogs bustled about on each side of the pop guns with their bristles out and pushed as hard as they could. The squirrels had some string around their tummies, which was threaded over the trigger, and they shouted, "One, two, three!" Then they ran as fast as they could in the opposite direction, pulling the triggers.

The rabbits ran and jumped on the cone-gun triggers, and the rest of the rabbits and squirrels kept loading the guns as fast as they could.

What a sight to behold. There were Ping-Pong balls shooting in all directions, and it looked like big hailstones raining down on the *bad badgers*.

All the badgers were growling, and Bosco was shouting in a really gruff, nasty voice, which made the rabbits and squirrels very scared.

"Keep going!" shouted Bosco. "We cannot let them stop us. We shall frighten them away if we have to."

Bundle was getting a bit upset, but he dared not show any weakness to Bosco. He growled as loudly as he could with the others, and they kept advancing on the little folk.

Sergeant Squirrel bashed his baton on the nearest thing he could find—which was unfortunately Maximus Mole, who had just stuck his head out—and shouted, "Listen up, all of you; don't be afraid. We shall have to use Plan B." Then he put his whistle in his mouth and blasted three times, waited a short beat, and blasted three more times. The squirrels in the oak tree did the same.

The little folk were frightened. Some could hardly move when they heard it until they saw others rushing about, and then they all started moving. Slopey Field had never ever seen so much activity and so many little folk.

The Wishing Wizard had awakened and was on one of his "reckies" (flyabouts) when all this was happening, and he saw Slopey Field. *Oh dear*, he thought, *I really do need to help the little folk.* He flourished his coat in a big swish and landed between Dooley and Henry.

"Can I join in? But shush, don't tell," he said as he put his finger to his lips.

And so it was.

Serena, Sally, and Sylvie Swan all joined the circle along with Oscar the Otter and Drake and Dyllis Duck. Rasta Rabbit had managed to get all his rabbit friends from all over the island to come, and they covered all the eastern side of Slopey Field. Sergeant Squirrel sent messages out to all the squirrels on the island, and he was very surprised at how many there were! They covered all the western side of Slopey Field. Oh, what a magnificent sight it was! When Henry saw that it was all coming together, he said to his group, "Right, that's it; join hands and wish and hope as hard as you possibly can."

Now all the little folk and the Wishing Wizard were holding hands, paws, claws, and wings in a great big circle all around the outside of Slopey Field. Heath the Hare and his cousins were running helter-skelter all around the outside of the circle to make sure there were no breaks in the chain. When Heath saw anyone slouching, he shouted, "Bottoms up," as he passed them, and the little folk stretched up straight and concentrated.

The little folk scrunched up their faces, shut their eyes, and started to hum, which got louder and louder until it built up to a really big sound. One or two opened their eyes and gasped, "Oh, oh!" It was a wondrous sight. Something was happening! The end of the rainbow was shimmering and shimmying, and it became hard to make out where the end of the rainbow was!

"It's working, it's working," said a few little voices, and they all tried harder and harder. Then they all saw that it was indeed working. Oh, it was beautiful. The little folk were amazed at this wonderful sight!

"Look!" shouted Mo, "The bottom of the rainbow is changing." And it was. It looked as if the sun had come out of the ground and was sending sun rays up to the sky.

"The rainbow is disappearing up and away!"

"Little swirls of colour are breaking away!" he sang. And they all joined in.

Eventually the bottom of the rainbow disappeared completely. It was a beautiful sight!

The *bad badgers* had become very, very upset that things were not going according to their plan. They stared at the end of the rainbow and saw the funny mist and even some sparkly stars, but they could not see the end of the rainbow. *Oh no*, they thought, *all our plans are not going to work, we are not going to get the gold.* And they turned around grumbling and growling, with their heads hung very low, and trundled off back to High Tower.

Henry turned to the Wishing Wizard and said, "Thank you for helping us; we know we could not have done it without you."

By this time all the little folk had seen that the Wishing Wizard was with them, and they heard what he was saying.

"On the contrary, dear Henry, I did nothing magical. I forgot my wands, so I could not do any magic. This all happened because you all wished and hoped so hard; that is what made the end of the rainbow disappear," said the Wishing Wizard.

"Could this really be true?" asked Hettie.

"I assure you, Hettie, that without my wands I cannot do special magic. My coat got wet last time I was out, and I had to wash it. I forgot to put my wands back into my big wand pocket," said the Wishing Wizard.

"Now, that is magic," said Henry.

And all the little folk shouted, "Hip, hip, hooray!"

The Wishing Wizard went on to tell them that he felt that all this was his fault, and he was very sorry that he had created High Tower. The badgers may not have had such big ideas if he had not.

"You look different, Wishing Wizard," said Miney.

"I know, I know," shouted Meenie. "He has the scarecrow's hat on!"

"Ah," said the Wishing Wizard, winking at Mo. "Well, I saw his hat, and I thought it would be better for me and would keep me dry and my ears warm. So I asked the scarecrow if he would swap with me, and he didn't say no, so we swapped. And he even winked at me, or at least I thought he did. But it could have been the sun shining off his little shiny button eyes."

Mo's little face lit up. "Told you," he shouted. "Scarecrow can wink." And they all fell about laughing.

The Wishing Wizard then told them that he would change things for the better, and then he did a big swish with his coat and disappeared.

"We had better not hold our breath waiting for the Wishing Wizard to do something, because he will probably forget," said Hettie. The Wishing Wizard heard this and felt very sad, and he was determined not to let them down again.

There was a huge celebration in Slopey Field for the rest of the day, and the rabbits started to teach some of the little folk their rabbit dance. Mo still could not get it right, and he kept bowling into folks.

The Wishing Wizard decided not to waste any time because he did not want to let the little folk down; he went back to the Blackish Mountains for his wands and set off to High Tower.

"Now, I need to be sure the weather is right to do this reversing magic," he said out loud to himself as he took a deep, deep breath and blew out three times. Each time he blew out, it formed a little puffy cloud like those little cotton wool clouds in the sky in summer.

"Good, good," he said. "The time is right. Now I hope I can remember the right order of the spell." Then he frowned and concentrated, and he waved four of his wands, because it had to be a strong spell. Then he started talking in a very funny language.

The following day, everyone was still in very high spirits and still laughing and dancing all day.

The Wishing Wizard returned in the blink of an eye and said, "I have been a very silly wizard, and I did not think it through properly when I granted that wish to the badgers. If you grant a wish to someone, it should only give pleasure and be of benefit. I have put this right now. The badgers do not have High Tower anymore. They will have to live as they always have, in their setts underground. And I promise you this: no one shall ever steal the gold from the end of the rainbow."

That night Dooley went out for his night foraging, and when he looked towards High Tower, it wasn't there. All he could see were three big pine trees where the tower used to be!

"Oh, wow," said Dooley out loud. "I'd better rush to tell all my friends in Slopey Field."

And that's how it all started in the first place!

XVII

SETTLING DOWN

Everything started to settle down in Rangseydale. Summer was approaching, and the little folk became very busy, foraging and collecting their things for saving. The Brockies were the main bankers for the island, and everyone trusted them. The renegade bankers that had tried to steal the gold from the end of the rainbow were not popular anymore, and no little folk used their services. They actually had to do more work and forage more for themselves. Dooley still talked to them because that was the kind of badger he was, but the rest of the little folk were very angry and avoided them.

"If someone does something as bad as they did, they cannot expect forgiveness so easily," said Hettie.

"I agree," said Henry, "but it is to be hoped that they have all learned a lesson and eventually become good badgers again."

"Meanwhile, we are happy, happy hedgehogs because there is still gold at the end of the rainbow!" shouted Mo. And they all started rolling and bowling just like any other lovely day on Slopey Field.

"I want to play marbles. I hope you haven't lost your marbles, Mo," said Meenie.

"No," said Mo, "I left them with the Brockies. I'll go and get them." And he turned to scuttle off to the Brockies' sett.

As he was leaving, Hettie said, "Is that what I think it is, Henry?"

"Yup," said Henry.

"Cool," said Hettie, getting the very last word!

And as they watched Mo sashaying down Slopey Field, they saw three very distinct dreadlocks swinging on his back.

Mo finally feels "cool!"

The End

For now

It is said that as soon as a rainbow starts to disappear, everyone knows the little folk are wishing and hoping. If you listen very carefully, you may even hear them humming.

Thanks to my wonderful "bling" readers; proofreader Maxine Conley; content readers—Warren Horner, Linda Watson, and Joanne Fisher; young "bling" readers Ellis Beaumont, Lilly Craig, Phoebe Cole, and Isobelle French—thanks for their smashing ideas!

Special thanks to all my friends who have supported and encouraged the writing of this book and to my family, who listened resolutely to my tales of the little folk.

And—as always—thanks to my wonderful husband, Warren, whose support over the years has been second to none and without whom Eenie, Meenie, Miney, and Mo and the little folk may never have saved the gold at the end of the rainbow.

Thank you, special human blings.

AUTHOR'S NOTE

I spent my childhood growing up in Nidderdale, North Yorkshire, England, surrounded by flowers and trees in fields and woods not unlike those on Big Island. I watched hedgehogs play, and squirrels run along branches, and lots of other little folk going about their business. I feel very privileged to have had these experiences. The first decade of life is the best decade. I now live in Pudsey with my husband and my little dog, who is called Dooley.

I value the insight of children untainted by the trials and tribulations of life and know that their ideas and views are worth their weight in gold, just like at the end of the rainbow.

I hope to write two more books based on Big Island. Plots are already decided. However, I plan to listen to children for their ideas and incorporate them, wherever possible, in the following books.

Also by Gilly Horner (as Gill Watson):   *SPANNER—A Dales Lad to Bomber Command and Back* (2011)

"No little folk were hurt in the writing of this book, nothing that a poultice would not fix anyway."

Made in the USA
Charleston, SC
10 December 2016